Murder at the Winter Games

Roy MacGregor

M&S

An M&S Paperback Original from
McClelland & Stewart Ltd.
The Canadian Publishers

For Justin and Jarret Evans, hockey-mad sons of Trent Evans, who buried the lucky loonie at centre ice, and of Laurel Evans, who puts up with the basement game that never ends.

The author is grateful to Doug Gibson, who thought up this series, and to Alex Schultz, who pulls it off.

Copyright © 2004 by Roy MacGregor

National Library of Canada Cataloguing in Publication

MacGregor, Roy, 1948–
  Murder at the winter games / Roy MacGregor.

(The Screech Owls series; 18)
ISBN 0-7710-5647-8

  I. Title. II. Series:

PS8575.G84M88 2004   jC813'.54   C2003-906819-6

We acknowledge the financial support of the Government of Canada through the Book Publishing Industry Development Program and that of the Government of Ontario through the Ontario Media Development Corporation's Ontario Book Initiative. We further acknowledge the support of the Canada Council for the Arts and the Ontario Arts Council for our publishing program.

Cover illustration by Gregory C. Banning
Typeset in Bembo by M&S, Toronto
Printed and bound in Canada

McClelland & Stewart Ltd.
The Canadian Publishers
481 University Ave.
Toronto, Ontario
M5G 2E9
www.mcclelland.com

1 2 3 4 5   08 07 06 05 04

TRAVIS LINDSAY COULD FEEL THE JELLY BEAN inside his nose.

It was green – the *perfect* colour, a delighted, red-faced Nish had shouted out to the rest of the Screech Owls. Perfect, he meant, for the Snot Shot.

Travis's assignment was simple. He was to plug his other nostril, tip his head back, and – with the help of his "aimer," Fahd – blow out so hard he sent the green jelly bean flying across the wide hotel ballroom. Longest Snot Shot wins.

Travis had never been so grossed out in his life.

But then, he had to admit, how else *should* one feel at the Gross-Out Olympics?

Nish was like a circus master, completely in charge. His big red face looked like it had been plugged into a wall socket. He was sweating, his black hair sticking to his forehead as if he'd just removed his helmet at the end of a hockey game. He was wearing his Screech Owls jersey, the big 44 and "Nishikawa" stitched across the back, holding a cordless microphone and standing centre stage, conducting the proceedings to the delight of every peewee team in attendance.

The Owls were in Park City, Utah, where the ski events at the Salt Lake City Winter Games were held. They had been invited to the Peewee Olympics, a week-long international hockey competition that included teams from most places in the world that played the game.

The Owls had been delighted to run into players they already knew from other tournaments. The Portland Panthers were there, with big Stu Yantha playing centre and little Jeremy Billings on defence. The Boston Mini-Bruins were there, and the Long Island Selects, the Detroit Wheels, the Vancouver Mountain, and even the dreaded Toronto Towers.

The competition was certain to be great, but the greatest thing of all was that the gold- and bronze-medal games were going to be played at the famous E Center, site of the glorious Canadian men's and women's victories in the 2002 Winter Games.

And real, genuine gold- and silver- and bronze-plated medals were going to be awarded to the first-, second-, and third-place finishers.

The Owls could not have been more excited. Sarah Cuthbertson and Samantha Bennett were going to play on the same ice surface that Cassie Campbell and Hayley Wickenheiser had skated on, where Jayna Hefford had picked up her own rebound and scored the winning goal in Canada's remarkable 3-2 victory over the American women.

Travis and his best friend, Wayne Nishikawa, were no different. Nish was already trying to convince Travis to try a "Mario Lemieux" and let a pass from Sarah slip between his legs so that Nish – like his hero (and "cousin") Paul Kariya – could score a goal while everyone else was certain Travis would be shooting.

The Screech Owls' goaltender, Jeremy Weathers, was going to play where his idol, Martin Brodeur, had performed so brilliantly when the Canadian men's team won 5-2, the final goal scored by one of Travis's favourite players, Joe Sakic.

The only Owl not so delighted – or at least pretending not to be – was Lars Johanssen, who said he felt ill every time he thought of the E Center and the shot from centre ice that went off Swedish goaltender Tommy Salo's glove, his head, and his back before landing in the net and giving little Belarus a 4-3 win and knocking Sweden, the early favourite, right out of the Olympics.

Here, too, was where Edmonton ice-maker Trent Evans had hidden his famous loonie at centre ice so both Canadian teams would have a little special luck – a story that had become such a legend in Canadian hockey that the lucky one-dollar coin was on permanent display at the Hockey Hall of Fame in Toronto.

Nish, of course, swore he would have something buried at centre ice to bring the Owls good luck. He would not, however, tell them what he planned.

"Just make sure it's not your boxer shorts," said Sam. "We don't want the ice to *melt*!"

Right now, Nish's mind was as far away from hockey and centre ice and a gold medal as it was possible to get.

He was running the Gross-Out Olympics, an idea he came up with on the long bus ride to Utah. Somehow – Travis didn't care to know the details – Nish had sold the Panthers and the Selects and the Towers on the idea since they were all staying in the same hotel.

And now, to great fanfare, the Gross-Out Olympics had begun. They would continue for the remainder of the hockey tournament, with Nish's version of the gold, silver, and bronze to be handed out the same day the hockey medals would be decided.

Travis, much to his surprise, proved to be extremely adept at the Snot Shot; the jelly bean would shoot across the room as hard as if he'd thrown it. Perhaps it was because he was so small and his tiny nose made the perfect bazooka for a jelly bean. Perhaps it was because he had good wind and could release it with such a snort. Perhaps it was because he figured he'd rather do the Snot Shot than any of the other ridiculous Gross-Out Olympic games Nish had come up with.

There was the Fly on the Wall event, in which each team had to select a player they would duct-tape to the wall, with Nish holding Mr. Dillinger's big old pocket watch to time who would stick the longest. Travis had been terrified they'd pick him, since he was one of the smallest, but the Owls had elected to go with little Simon Milliken, who was not only slightly smaller than Travis but had also readily volunteered.

Sam was up for the Alphabet Burp — a test to see which contestant could go deepest into the alphabet burping out each letter clearly enough for everyone else to understand. Sam, who seemed able to burp at will, had graciously agreed when the team chose her as their entry, though she insisted, "Nish is a better burper — *too bad he doesn't know the alphabet!*"

There was the Slurp, where a player had to pull pantyhose over his or her head and eat a bowl of Jell-O by forcing the jiggling dessert through the nylon. Sarah insisted only she could do it, as she was the only Screech Owl who had brought pantyhose to Utah, and she had no intention of letting anyone else put them on over their head — particularly not Nish, who had been boasting he could eat more Jell-O than any peewee player in the world.

There was the Chubby Bunny, in which the competitors had to show how many marshmallows they could stuff in their mouths and still say the words "Chubby Bunny" clearly enough to be understood. Much to everyone's surprise, the Owls' leader so far in the practice sessions had not been big Andy Higgins or even Gordie Griffith, the team's best eater, but Jesse Highboy, who was considered the lightest eater on the entire team. Jesse had managed to cram thirteen marshmallows into the sides of his cheeks and still say "Chubby Bunny" with great clarity. So he was the automatic choice for that event.

There was the Cricket Spit, the mere thought of which turned Travis's stomach. Nish and Data had gone to a nearby pet-supply store and purchased a box of live crickets, claiming the team had a chameleon for a mascot. Nish was still searching for an Owl willing to see how many crickets they could land in a garbage pail by forming a funnel with their tongue and firing the little bugs from a specified distance.

There was the Frozen T-Shirt contest, in which tournament T-shirts were to be soaked, then frozen, then tossed, rock solid, into the arms of players who then had to get them over their heads. First one to get completely into an ice-cold shirt wins. Dmitri, to everyone's surprise, had volunteered for the contest. "My family originally came from Siberia," he told the Owls, "so we're used to putting on frozen clothes."

For the grand finale, Nish said, he had devised the greatest event of all — a game he would neither name nor describe but one he claimed would "separate the men from the boys, the women from the girls, the brave from the cowards, and the winners from the losers."

"*Ready!*" Nish barked into the microphone.

Travis stretched out on the floor and laid his head back. Fahd had his hands cupped and ready, aiming Travis like a cannon for the big shot. A shot too low would hit the floor too soon; a shot too high would be wasted. It had to be exactly the right trajectory for the best distance.

Next to him, Jeremy Billings, the Portland Panthers' Snot Shot competitor, laid his head back into the hands of big Yantha.

The two remaining competitors in the event, Travis and Jeremy, looked like bookends, both small, both fair-haired, both quick to smile. They had been, by far, the best of the shooters, each winning his early rounds handily.

"*Remember,*" Nish shouted, his red face dripping sweat, "*this is for the gold medal in the Snot Shot!*"

"*Go, Trav!*" Data shouted from the sidelines.

"*Jeremy rules!*" one of the Panthers shouted.

"*Get set!*" roared Nish into the microphone.

Travis closed his eyes and pinched tight the empty side of his nose. He put all his attention on the expulsion of air. The aiming he'd leave to Fahd, who claimed to have worked out the physics with Data and knew exactly what trajectory the jelly bean should take.

"*GO!*" Nish screamed, the mike screeching with feedback as he practically shoved it down his throat.

With every ounce of his existence, Travis blew. He heard his own hard burst of breath, heard also Jeremy Billings's wind explode from his lungs. He opened his eyes and waited for the telltale sounds.

Ping! Ping!

Skip! Skip!

He heard the two jelly beans land on the parquet floor at almost exactly the same time: it was impossible to say which had landed first or which had landed farthest from the two human cannons.

He would hear the jelly beans sliding, spinning . . . then silence.

A roar went up from the Portland Panthers.

Travis knew instantly. He had lost. Jeremy had blown his jelly bean farther.

"*Jeremy!*" one of the Panthers shouted out.

8

"*Panthers rule!*"

"*Je-re-my! Je-re-my!*"

Travis pushed himself up into a sitting position. He could feel Fahd's hand gripping his shoulder.

"I screwed up," Fahd was saying. "I screwed up. I aimed you too high, Trav."

Travis turned and looked at his friend. Fahd looked forlorn, like he'd just blown a breakaway in a real tournament.

Travis couldn't help but laugh. "Fahd!" he said. "Get a grip — *it's a jelly bean!*"

"I'm so sorry," Fahd continued, not even listening. "It's all my fault."

Other hands were on Travis's back now. Sarah's hand, patting. Sam's hand, slamming. Dmitri. Lars. Liz. Data. Andy. Simon. Jesse. Willie. Derek. Gordie. Jenny. Wilson. Jeremy.

"Good try, Trav," Sarah was saying.

There was another hand reaching for him over the Owls. Travis took Jeremy Billings's hand and gripped tight.

"Great try," Billings said, smiling sheepishly.

"Congratulations," said Travis, laughing.

"Maybe we'll meet again in the *real* gold-medal contest," Billings said.

Travis nodded, but before he could speak, the public-address system crackled and sputtered and Nish — who clearly considered his Gross-Out Olympics the true gold-medal challenge of the tournament – was well into his announcement.

"*Lay-deeees and gennnnull-mennnnn . . .*," Nish roared in his absurd Elvis Presley voice. "Thank you . . . thank you very much . . . The results of the gold-medal event in the Snot Shot . . . the winner, *by a nose . . .*"

2

"*WEIRD*," SAID SAM.

"Weirdest thing I've ever seen in my life."

Travis could not disagree. But he dared not say anything – even whispering was dangerous. They could so easily be caught, and he had no appetite for going through the embarrassment of explaining why he and Sam and Sarah were hiding behind the potted plants in the most elegant hotel lobby in all of Park City.

They had sneaked into the Summit Watch, a luxury hotel so perfectly situated that guests merely had to step outside the door to line up for the lifts taking skiers high up into the mountains.

They had come here because Sam, who would talk to anyone, had been gabbing to one of the players on the Hollywood Stars – a peewee team from California that was a complete unknown to all the other teams gathered at Park City.

The kids had heard rumours about this team. It was supposed to be filled with the children of movie stars and rock stars, the richest peewee team in the world, with its own private rink, its own luxury bus, and – though no one truly believed it – its own charter jet for distant tournaments.

Sam, who read *People* magazine the way some people study the Bible, had picked the player out immediately as he came strolling down Main Street with his parents. The kid was decked out in the nicest team track suit the Owls had ever seen. It was pitch black, but with a sun exploding on the back, and, in what appeared to be solid-gold thread, "Hollywood Stars" stitched across the shoulders as well as a bright gold number on the right arm and the player's first name on the left.

The player Sam talked to was called Keddy, according to his arm. Keddy confirmed not only that they were the Hollywood team Sam had been reading about, but that their star player, Brody Prince, was coming in late with his parents and was expected at the Summit Watch hotel within the hour.

Hiding out in the lobby had been all Sam's idea. She had, Travis told her, "stars in her eyes," but even he couldn't help but feel the curiosity, the excitement, the anticipation of hanging around the lobby waiting for the arrival of the Prince family.

Troy Prince, Brody's father, had been a huge rock star before going into acting, and now he was one of the biggest screen names in Hollywood. Brody's mother, Isabella Val d'Or, was a super-model and sometime actress, and was said to have been married at one point to Michael Jackson. She had, *People* magazine claimed, and Sam repeated, a weakness for bizarre men.

If Michael Jackson was weird, he had little on Troy Prince, who had been arrested so many times even the gossip columnists had lost track. The father had been arrested for bar fights, for carrying concealed handguns, for causing disruptions on planes, for beating up photographers, and, once, when he'd been a rock star, for appearing nude on a hotel balcony as thousands of fans gathered below to cheer him – only to be mooned by their idol.

As the years had gone by, and Troy Prince's fabulous wealth had mounted thanks to his music and films, he had become more law-abiding but no less weird. He appeared at the Oscars in dark sunglasses and a surgical mask. He wore rubber gloves when greeting fans for fear he'd pick up germs off their hands. He once, Sam claimed, had gone a solid year without speaking to a soul and, at one point during this quiet year, had even financed a multi-million-dollar silent movie intended to cash in on nostalgia for the early years of film but which had bombed horribly. It hardly mattered. Troy Prince was now a billionaire from his song royalties and investments.

But his strangest quirk of all – according to *People* magazine – didn't strike Travis as peculiar at all.

He was a hockey nut.

Troy Prince was born in England, not Canada. He grew up with soccer, not hockey. But apparently one night, before he was to play a sold-out concert in Chicago, he stayed after a sound check to watch a hockey match between the Blackhawks and the Toronto Maple Leafs, and got completely hooked on the game.

He'd become so obsessed he'd even gone to the Wayne Gretzky Fantasy Camp – a week-long hockey school for adults – and had hired a former NHLer to help him learn to skate better. He'd then built an NHL-sized rink in Hollywood with dressing rooms equipped with a sound system in every stall and hot tubs instead of showers.

And when his son Brody had shown an interest in the game, he put together a team of youngsters, completely outfitted them, and then hired a former NHL coach, Buzz Blundell, to teach the kids the fundamentals.

According to the rumour, Blundell had three assistant coaches, all with pro-hockey backgrounds. One was said to be a special video coach who was hooked up to Blundell via headphones and who stayed in a large trailer in the parking lot, where he could monitor a series of cameras set up around the rink. Here, he was able to break down video replays, analyze them, and then instantly report back to Blundell during the actual game, so the head coach could make adjustments on the fly.

For three years the team had practised in secret, playing only scrimmages against themselves, but now, this winter, the Hollywood Stars had started showing up at tournaments.

And they had yet to lose a single game.

"Weird," said Sam again.

Weird indeed.

The three Screech Owls were still hidden behind the rhododendrons and potted palm trees, Sam down on her knees peeking through the legs of the baby grand piano, when the Prince family limousines pulled up.

Travis had seen a display like this once before: in Washington, when the president of the United States came to watch his son, Chase, play in the final game of the International Goodwill Peewee Championship. But this put the fuss over the president to shame. The Princes had a police motorcycle escort. They had a forward car – a black Lincoln SUV – filled with a private security force that piled out as if they were marines moving in on an enemy encampment. They were all big, beefy men with suspicious bulges behind their left arms where Travis figured they must keep their holstered handguns.

The security force swept the street and the front entrance, checking for whatever it is security people look for, then moved quickly through the revolving doors into the lobby.

Travis was certain they were about to be found and, for all he knew, arrested.

But the security force seemed to assume that inside the hotel all was secure. They moved straight to the elevator to check out the rooms as the Prince family entered the hotel behind them.

Travis heard Sam and Sarah gasp.

He leaned out a little further and caught sight of the best-looking young kid he had ever seen: jet-black hair, green eyes, a slightly crooked nose, and, already, the signs of widening shoulders and developing arms.

Behind the kid entered a woman who seemed taller than any of the men around her and had the undivided attention of every one of them. She was extraordinarily beautiful and moved across the room with her shoulders back and her head held high. Her hair bounced as she walked, and her eyes took everything in yet settled on nothing.

Struggling to keep up were staff pushing luggage carts piled high with suitcases – huge silver suitcases that looked, to Travis, as if they should be holding the Stanley Cup, not clothes and shoes.

Behind the luggage carts came a man who was obviously Troy Prince. He wore dark wrap-around glasses and had a white surgical mask over his mouth, and he was dressed in a dark suit with a rich white silk scarf hanging loosely around his neck.

He was also carrying a hockey stick.

In all his life, Travis had never seen anything so out of place as this hockey stick in the hand of this man. A hockey stick held by a hand in a rubber surgical glove.

"Weird," Travis repeated.

"Weird."

3

TRAVIS HAD A GUT FEELING HE WOULD HAVE A good tournament.

He was standing at the head of the line, helmet pressed to the glass above the gate leading onto the ice. The Zamboni had just gone off, the ice was still glistening wet under the lights of the Park City arena, and the attendant was closing the chute doors and signalling that the teams could now come on.

Travis was first, just as he liked it. He felt his skate touch the ice, heard the wonderful little sizzle as he dug in hard with his right leg and pushed off, giving his ankle a small flick as the blade left the surface.

Everything had gone perfectly. Mr. Dillinger had all the skates sharpened and stacked in the middle of the dressing room. There had been fabulous jokes about the stink rising from Nish's equipment bag and lots of talk about the Hollywood Stars and their bizarre owner.

Travis had felt good dressing. He had kissed the inside of his sweater, right behind the "C" for captain, as he pulled his jersey over his head.

Muck had made one of his shortest speeches ever: "There's no 'I' in 'team' – you got that, Nishikawa?"

Nish had looked up from his festering equipment bag, red face grimacing: "There's *two* 'I's in 'Nishikawa,' coach."

"Sometimes it seems like there's nothing but 'I's in 'Nishikawa,'" joked Sarah from the far corner, causing Muck to smile and Nish to stick out his tongue.

They were up against the Detroit Wheels, a big, tough peewee team the Owls had last met for the championship of the Big Apple International, a tournament Nish claimed he had won single-handedly by scoring on his "Bure" move. He had flipped the puck over the net from behind and skated out in front in time to cuff it out of the air and in for the overtime victory.

Travis hit the crossbar on his first warm-up shot – a good sign that the tournament would go well for him – but he still felt nervous. *Nice* nervous, not *bad* nervous.

Tournaments were different from any other kind of play. Travis wasn't sure why, but in the first game of a tournament it always felt as if his breath came a little quicker, his legs seemed a little more rubbery, his eyes moved just a fraction of a second behind the play.

Tournaments tended to have a little jump to them that was missing in league play. And the other teams and players were generally strangers – you had no automatic fix on them. Travis sometimes marvelled at how the Owls could play a team only a few times in league action and he'd have a sense of who was dangerous and who could be beaten either by speed or puck-handling. Eventually, he wouldn't even have to see the numbers on the other players; he could tell just by body language who was where when he was on the ice and what they were capable of doing. A defenceman might be back on his heels and make it easy to poke a puck through his skates. A forward might be a lazy backchecker or a sloppy puck-handler. A goalie might go down too much or have a strong glove hand the Owls' shooters should try to avoid.

In a way, Travis thought, hockey was an endless scouting report, constantly being revised in a player's brain – often without the player even being aware he was picking up such information.

But in a tournament everything was fresh and new and all the players had to prove themselves as if for the first time. Travis knew it would be just a matter of a few shifts before the other team realized that Dmitri's speed was a killer, that Sarah was a great playmaker, and that Travis was absolutely ferocious in the corners.

They'd also soon learn that the big, loud, red-faced number 44 on the Owls' defence was not one player but two or three different players. He could be lazy and seem unimportant on the ice. He could be silly and self-centred, always trying to make the hero play. Or, as Travis liked him best, he could be a totally driven team player, determined to do whatever it took to win.

Travis knew the players didn't see that third Nish too often – but once they did, they never forgot it.

The Wheels were big, and often played dirty. Travis was slashed right off the opening faceoff, but the referee either didn't see it or decided to let it go. His right forearm and wrist were numb and tingling, and when Sarah kicked the puck to him he found the arm had no strength. The puck skittered right off his stick and into the feet of the big winger who had slashed him. The winger kicked the puck off the boards, danced around Travis, picked it up, and broke in fast on Samantha and Fahd, the Owls' starting defence pairing.

Fahd made the mistake of playing the puck, not the man. He stabbed to poke-check the player only to have him neatly tuck the puck back, out of harm's way, and then flick it ahead, past Fahd.

It was an instant two-on-one, with Sam trying to stay between the two rushing Wheels and Jenny Staples, who'd been named by Muck to start in nets, playing the shooter.

The puck carrier decided to pass. Sam brilliantly fell and blocked it with her upper body, but the puck bounced off her shoulder pads straight back to the passer and – just as Jenny was sliding across the crease to play the one-timer from the other side – he was able to slam it into a wide-open net.

Wheels 1, Owls 0.

Travis was near tears on the bench. His arm was screaming in pain and his bad play had coughed up the puck and led to a goal in the first minute of the first game of the tournament.

He felt something being squeezed in between him and Dmitri. He looked down. It was ice, all neatly bagged in plastic and chopped up small so it would pack around his arm.

Good old Mr. Dillinger. Always prepared. No one had even said a word about the dirty slash, but everyone knew. No one on the bench was going to blame Travis for something that wasn't his fault.

Derek took the next couple of shifts for Travis. He sent Dmitri in on a breakaway at one point, but Dmitri clipped his signature backhander off the crossbar and high into the safety net.

Nish pretended not to see the big winger who had slashed Travis and backed into him, acting like he was playing the puck on the stick of another Detroit forward. The big winger went down hard and play had to be called for the trainer to come onto the ice and help the Detroit player to the bench.

Nish winked at Travis as he came off the ice. Travis smiled. He was ready to play again.

Andy Higgins tied the game 1-1 early in the second with a wicked slapper that hit the Detroit goalie's glove and both posts before going into the net.

By now, Travis had full feeling back in his arm. It was still aching, and he was icing it between shifts, but his strength had come back and he was determined to make up for the opening goal.

Sarah, who was playing wonderfully, won a faceoff in the Owls' end and fired the puck back behind the goal, where Nish picked it up and dodged the first check by bouncing the puck off the back of the net as the winger roared past him.

Nish looked up ice, his eyes calm, his face so expressionless it seemed to Travis his friend had gone into one of his trances. He could play, at times, as if hypnotized, as if something else were controlling him.

Nish moved out over the blueline, deftly stick-handling past the opposing centre. He flipped a neat pass to Dmitri by the right boards, and Dmitri fired the puck back almost before it reached him, causing a pinching Detroit defence-man to turn so fast in panic that he lost an edge and went down.

Nish broke over centre just as the ice opened up to the Owls' rush. The Wheels had only one defenceman back now, and both Detroit wingers were hustling to get back to cover.

It was, for a moment, a three-on-one, with Travis, Sarah, and Nish, the puck carrier.

Nish came in hard over the Detroit blueline, faked a slapshot, and slipped a beautiful drop pass to Sarah, who looped quickly inside the blue-line as the one Detroit winger sailed harmlessly past her.

As Sarah circled and looked up, Travis moved into the slot, while Nish, digging hard, came in from the other side.

Sarah sent a perfect lead pass to Travis.

Trusting in his arm, he fired the puck instantly, one-timing it off the ice so fast that the Detroit goaltender, who had seen the play develop, had no time to do anything but position himself and hope for the best.

He hoped in vain.

Travis's shot went up hard to the short side, over the goaltender's blocker, and in off the crossbar.

Owls 2, Wheels 1.

This time when Travis went off the ice it was to backslaps and high-fives and, that rarity of rarities, a quick neck massage from Muck, who said not a word. Nothing needed to be said: the coach's touch said it all.

Only Nish spoke, and it was to remind Travis

of something they'd talked about before the tournament.

"You had a chance to do a Lemieux there, buddy," he said. "Just let that pass go through your legs, and I woulda Kariya-ed it into the empty side."

"We scored, didn't we?" said Travis, a little annoyed.

"*You* scored," Nish said, raising his face mask and pushing a towel hard into his eyes.

Travis shook his head and said nothing. Nish was being an idiot. *Did it not count because I scored it?* Travis wondered. *Would they have awarded two points if Nish had been able to recreate the famous Olympic goal?*

The Wheels tried to come back in the third and almost scored on a rebound late in the period, only to have Nish dive in across the crease, knocking both Jenny and the puck out of the way. The Wheels called for a penalty, claiming Nish had closed his hand on the puck, but the referee would have none of it. In the entire game, he had yet to call a single penalty.

With no danger of whistles, the Detroit team turned nasty as the game wound down. There were slashes and spears and elbows on every play.

"No retaliation," Muck ordered. "They play their game. We play ours. Understand?"

The players on the bench nodded. They understood. They knew Muck would have nothing to do with this style of play, even if it meant losing.

The Wheels keyed on Nish, who was clearly the most dangerous of the Owls on the ice. They hit him on every play and tried to get him to fight after every whistle. But Nish kept that faraway look in his eyes and treated the Wheels as if they weren't even there. Finally, with the clock winding down in the final minute, the Wheels began running Nish at random.

He used their strategy against them, waiting for them to charge and then stepping quickly out of the way as one after another slammed into the boards. Then he took off, carrying the puck as if he were all alone on the ice. One Wheel tried to take his feet out from under him, but Nish just kicked the slash away with his shin pad.

He came up over centre, wound up, and crushed a shot from well outside the Detroit blueline that simply blew by the astonished goaltender.

Owls 3, Wheels 1.

The horn sounded with the Detroit team still running the Owls, but there was no retaliation. Muck ordered his team off the ice immediately while he went over to offer his hand to the opposing coach and have a few quiet words with the referee.

The Owls fell into their dressing room exhausted, sore, but happy. Helmets crashed into lockers, sticks clattered over the floor, gloves landed everywhere but where they belonged, and several of the players lay down flat on the floor, as Nish always did, and raised their legs onto the benches.

Nish liked to say it was to "get some blood back to my brain." And Sam usually added, "We'll need a massive transfusion for that, then."

"I hope we never see that ref again!" said Sarah.

"He was pitiful," said Simon.

"That guy who slashed you should have been thrown out of the tournament," Jesse Highboy said to Travis.

"I'm okay now," said Travis, but his arm was throbbing. The pain was rushing back.

Mr. Dillinger came into the dressing room and tossed a fresh ice pack at him. Travis took it, smiling.

The door opened again a second later. It was the official scorer, smiling. "Good game, Owls – we picked number 44 as MVP."

The Owls all cheered as one.

The man looked around the room, finding Nish still with his legs up on the bench. "Just want to double-check the spelling of your name, son . . ."

"It's N-*I*-S-H-*I*-K-A-W-A," Nish told him.

Then he smiled, big red face beaming.

"That's with *two* 'I's."

4

TRAVIS HAD OFTEN HEARD HIS PARENTS USE THE phrase "fly on a wall" – but this was more like "hockey player on a wall."

Simon Milliken was hanging two feet off the floor in the ballroom. He was surrounded by other Owls standing on chairs and working furiously to rip duct tape off several rolls and use it to plaster Simon's legs, arms, torso, and even head to the wall.

Next to Simon was little Jeremy Billings, being similarly taped up by the Portland Panthers. Another tiny player was being taped by the Detroit Wheels, another by the Toronto Towers, one by the Boston Mini-Bruins, one by the Long Island Selects, and one by the Vancouver Mountain.

Round Two of the Gross-Out Olympics was under way!

"*Fifteen more seconds!*" Nish barked into his cordless microphone.

"*Ten seconds!*"

Hands worked furiously. The big room was echoing with the sound of tearing and ripping as the teams tore off strips of duct tape and slapped them over every part of the players' bodies to secure them more firmly to the wall. There was tape over pants and T-shirts and socks and bare skin – and even tape over tape wherever possible.

"*Five seconds!*"

Travis could barely hear himself think for the furious ripping of the sticky tape.

"*Four . . . three . . . two . . . ONE!*

"*STOP TAPING!*"

Instantly, the taping stopped, all except for one final tear from down towards the Vancouver Mountain team, which caused a quick round of friendly boos from the other teams.

"*Stand back!*" Nish ordered.

All the players moved back – except, of course, for those players now plastered to the wall.

Travis giggled when he saw their handiwork. Simon and Jeremy and the others looked like they were floating in outer space against the dark wall of the ballroom, their bodies merely an outline beneath haphazard strips of silver duct tape.

Nish had Mr. Dillinger's big pocket watch in his hand and was now counting out how long they lasted. "*Fifteen seconds!*" he called out.

He was standing dead centre, the players taped to the wall to one side of him, the cheering teams on the other.

"*Thirty seconds!*"

The first sound of tape giving way came from Travis's left. It brought a loud groan of denial from the assembled members of the Detroit Wheels. The groaning, however, was good-natured – the Wheels seemed a lot friendlier off the ice.

Travis watched the scene unfold in slow motion: first the player's right arm came away, then, with the shift in weight, his right leg began to strain at the tape and, very slowly, pull away from the wall.

The Wheels groaned again in unison.

"*Forty-five seconds!*"

Nish had barely announced the new time when another player began to come unstuck, this time the Vancouver Mountain's competitor. The Vancouver team booed their own player – whereupon they, and everyone else in the room, began to laugh.

Travis turned, shaking his head – and then he saw that there was an eighth peewee hockey team in the ballroom.

The Hollywood Stars!

They had filed in so quietly no one had noticed them. But there was no mistaking them, not in their spectacular black-and-gold track suits with the sun exploding on the back.

Nor was there any mistaking Brody Prince, who stood with feet apart, his fists jabbed into jacket pockets, right in the middle of the group. Without his followers and his fancy track suit,

Brody Prince would still have stood out from everyone else in the room. The long jet-black hair, the flashing green eyes, the look that said "Hollywood" even before you saw the gold letters across his back spelling it out. Behind the team stood two large men – bodyguards, Travis presumed, for the "star" of the Hollywood Stars. He shook his head, appalled.

Suddenly there was a huge ripping noise from the other direction. Travis spun around just as the Wheels' player peeled off the wall and fell to thundering applause and cheers from his own teammates. The little player was laughing and taking it well.

"*One minute!*"

The Wheels player was barely down when the Vancouver player came away and plummeted, to wild boos and backslaps from his teammates.

Then a small girl from the Selects team tore away and fell, followed by a skinny kid from the Mini-Bruins.

There were only three players still sticking: a slim girl from the Toronto Towers, Jeremy Billings from the Panthers, and the Owls' own Simon Milliken.

"*One-fifteen!*" Nish called out.

Simon's left arm tore away, causing a loud groan of disappointment from the Owls.

"*One-thirty!*"

The girl's head and shoulders came unstuck, the weight causing the rest of the tape to stretch dangerously close to breaking.

Jeremy Billings's right arm and left leg pulled free, almost sending him into a spin.

There were no more groans, no more boos, no more cheers – it seemed not a breath was being taken by anyone in the room, particularly not by the three still sticking to the wall.

"*One-forty-five!*"

Simultaneously, Jeremy Billings and the girl from the Towers tumbled to the floor.

Simon's other arm broke free, then his shoulders, and he sagged like a rag doll, his legs somehow still holding.

"*Two minutes!*"

A huge cheer went up from the Owls. Simon held another ten seconds, then fell happily into the arms of his teammates.

"*Layyyyyyyyy-dddddiessss 'n' gennnnnull-mun,*" Nish began. "*Gold medal in the Fly on the Wall event – the Screech Owls! Silver medal – a tie! Toronto Towers and Portland Panthers!*"

Andy and Derek had little Simon up on their shoulders and were walking him around in triumph. The entire room was cheering the three medal winners.

Nish, his face swollen with pride, walked around high-fiving anyone who would raise a hand. He walked deliberately over to the

Hollywood Stars, not one of whom had said a word or, for that matter, even smiled.

"If you guys would like to join in," said Nish in a moment of unexpected generosity, "we'd be glad to have you in the Gross-Out Olympics. We've only done two events."

He spoke directly to Brody Prince, who stared down at Nish as if he were some foreign object he'd just found in his soup.

"We're here to win a tournament," said Prince, "not make asses of ourselves." And with that the entire Hollywood Stars team turned and began to file out of the room.

The ballroom was completely silent. No one spoke. Nish looked red enough to burst, his mouth moving helplessly in search of words.

Sam spoke for him.

"That's funny," she yelled after the closing door, "'cause you just did!"

5

THEY AWOKE IN THE ARCTIC.

At least that's the way it seemed. Fahd was the first to notice that ice had formed on the inside of the hotel windows. He got up, melted it off with the fleshy part of his hand, then used a towel to open up a porthole for the kids in room 323 to peer out onto Park City's Main Street.

It was freezing. Snow had fallen earlier in the night, but then the real chill had arrived and it had turned, strange as it might sound, too cold to snow. Cars were grinding up the street, their tires frozen square where they had flattened as the car sat overnight. Other drivers, more frustrated, were trying to get their car engines just to turn over and start, the engines whining for a bit, then slowing to complete silence as the frozen batteries gave up. The street was filled with exhaust that could not rise in the cold, making it seem as if a huge grey cloud had wrapped the town tight against the mountains.

"I'm staying in bed," Nish announced from under two comforters and three pillows, one of which he had stolen in the night from Travis.

"We're going on that tour," Fahd said.

"What tour?" Nish mumbled from beneath his pillows.

"Muck has signed us up to tour the town and see the old jail and the tunnels."

"Wow!" Nish mumbled sarcastically from under his mound of covers. "Maybe tomorrow morning we can go somewhere and watch paint dry!"

"Get up," Travis told his best friend. "It'll be fun."

Travis knew it would be. Muck was maybe a bit too much of a history buff at times, but his tours always turned out to be interesting. Muck knew better than to bore a group of twelve-year-olds with a military analysis of the Civil War, but he knew if he took them to a real Civil War battle-ground and let them loose around the cannons and monuments, the kids would all enjoy it. Even Nish.

They gathered in the lobby. Mr. Dillinger did his usual head count and then they all filed out into the bitter cold. Travis's nose locked solid the second he tried to breathe through it. Thank heaven they weren't having the Snot Shot outside on a day like this, he thought, smiling to himself. This was a day for breathing through the mouth. But even then the air was so frigid it stabbed into his lungs.

The Owls hurried to the tour centre a couple of blocks down the street. Several times Data's wheelchair got stuck in the snow and the team had to lift him over banks and drifts. They were grateful when they reached the tour centre just to get back inside into some heat. Simon Milliken's glasses fogged up the second the door closed behind them and he stood off in a corner wiping them clear with his scarf while the team waited for the tour to begin.

A very old man came in the door behind them, stomping his feet and coughing terribly from the cold. Travis wondered if he was going on the tour as well or had simply come in to warm up.

The old man began unbundling himself, first taking off a large fur hat, then unbuttoning an old coat that looked as if it weighed more than the man himself. He coughed a bit more, then cleared his throat, looked up and smiled.

"You must be the Screech Owls."

The old man was Ebenezer Durk and he was the official tour guide. He must have been well into his eighties, thought Travis, certainly older than Travis's grandfather back home in Tamarack. He had long, wispy white hair, had nicked himself shaving, and had a long white moustache that he'd waxed and twirled until it looked like a smile above the smile already on his old face.

If it was possible to look old and young at the same time, Ebenezer Durk had managed it. He seemed to creak as he moved. He was hunched and thin, and his clothes hung from him. His face was deeply creased and hollow, the skin white as the snow that lay piled along the sidewalks where it had been ploughed and pushed back from the street.

And yet his eyes danced with a childlike mischief when he looked at the Owls. His smile never faded, and his outlandish moustache seemed to signal a joke even before he spoke.

Travis liked him at once.

To Muck's great delight, Ebenezer Durk was one of those rare teachers who could bring history to life. When he told stories of Park City's past – the saloons, the shootings, the rough life of the miners, the fires, the crazy characters – they seemed as real as if he were telling them about something that happened only last evening.

Ebenezer Durk had been born in Park City to a miner and his wife and had lived here all his life. He could remember when the theatre roof caved in after a terrible snowstorm. He could recall the time the mail plane crashed into the mountainside near town, and how the townsfolk had raced out into the storm and saved the pilot and then gathered up all the mail that had been scattered up and down the mountain.

And he knew, personally, people who had been thrown in the jail.

The jail fascinated Nish – perhaps because his teammates were always telling him he was going to end up in one. The Park City jail had been kept just as it had been in the 1920s, a dark dungeon-like hole beneath the sheriff's office, with the prisoners' scratchings still on the wall and the doors still capable of clanging shut as if they were cutting off the world forever.

"My daddy was here for six months," Ebenezer Durk told them.

The Owls stared back in wonder. For what? *Murder?*

"I used to bring him his meals," the old man continued. "The sheriff would let me come down and slip a tray of soup and bread under the door and I'd wait until he was finished. Then I'd hurry home to my mother."

It was Fahd who finally asked. "Why was he here?"

The old man smiled, eyes sparkling. "I'll show you."

They crossed the street and walked up the other side until they came to an old building. Ebenezer Durk led them around to the back, where horses had once been stabled.

The heat of the old building had caused the snow to melt and flow down onto the roof of the stables, where it had dripped off the eaves and frozen into icicles so long they reached the ground.

"Neat!" said Sarah.

"They look like prison bars," said Fahd.

"I'm gonna get a picture," Data said.

They had to wait while Fahd helped Data get his camera out and take a shot of the spectacular icicles. Travis tried to make a snowball while he waited, but the snow wouldn't pack. He headed back towards the side of the building that had melted the snow, figuring there might be packy snow along the walls, but it was still too soft and the snowballs broke in his hands.

He was facing back to the street just as two men turned the corner and came towards the stable. There were other people out on the street, all dressed in ski clothes and heading for the lifts, but these men seemed to be dressed for a business meeting. The two men wore long, dark, and very expensive-looking coats, and each had a large black tuque turned down to his eyes, with a dark scarf wrapped around his mouth and neck.

All Travis could see were the eyes. And yet he thought he recognized one of them. Something about a hotel lobby . . . Yes, the Summit Watch hotel lobby! One of them, for certain, was a bodyguard for the Princes. Travis had seen him again when the Hollywood Stars showed up for the duct-tape event.

A moment later, the two men turned away and retreated to the street. Travis went back to the rest of the Owls, thought about saying something, but decided there was no point. The two men had just taken a wrong turn. It was obvious from how quickly they'd turned around and left.

Fahd was putting away Data's camera and the rest of the team was pushing towards the doors of the old stables.

Ebenezer Durk had opened a large padlock on a heavy black door, which Muck and Mr. Dillinger then helped him pry open.

"I don't very often take anyone here," said the old man, chuckling to himself.

He lit three lanterns, handing one to Muck, one to Mr. Dillinger, and taking one himself as he led the way down through a trapdoor to a ladder that seemed to lead to a black, bottomless pit.

"Are you sure . . . ?" Jeremy asked.

"*I'M GONNA DIE!*" Nish squealed in mock terror.

"We should be so lucky," Sam shot back.

Ebenezer Durk stopped at the bottom of the ladder, the lantern casting an eerie glow about his white face as he turned to talk to the shivering Owls.

"There are secret tunnels that run all up and down Main Street," he told them. "They're dangerous, and most of them have been closed off, but I can show you where the bootleggers operated."

"Bootleggers?" asked Fahd.

"People who sell alcohol illegally," Muck explained.

"But there's a liquor store just down the street," Fahd protested.

Ebenezer Durk laughed so hard he began to choke. He caught his breath and smiled at Fahd.

"Alcohol was illegal in this state for most of my life," he said. "But that didn't mean you couldn't get it. There was a lot more money to be made in bootlegging than in mining, let me tell you."

"You sound like you're talking from experience," said Muck.

The old man's eyes twinkled in the flickering light. "You bet I am, sir," he said. "You guessed why my daddy spent that winter in jail."

The tunnels, many of them blocked off entirely, a few of them still passable, had been built by the bootleggers. The tunnels allowed them to move about undetected by the police. They were also perfect for storing the illegal alcohol and, most importantly, provided the bootleggers with a variety of handy escape routes should the law-enforcement officers ever find their secret, hidden centre of operation.

Ebenezer Durk led them up a tunnel to a dark basement that Travis figured must be high on

Main Street. Here he showed them where the still had been for the manufacture of "moonshine" whiskey, and he told them a long story of how the police knew the illegal still was somewhere around here and had set up a watch to make sure there would be no deliveries to the hotels farther down the street.

"My daddy had a brilliant idea, though," Ebenezer told them. "He knew he couldn't take it down by horse and wagon – the authorities would be sure to stop and search him – but he could still do it by wagon."

"A wagon with no horses?" Sarah asked.

The old man chuckled. "Not exactly, my dear – a wagon and one very small boy."

He waited a moment for it to sink in.

"I had my little red wagon," he said, laughing, "and my daddy would plunk down a keg in it, wrap it in a burlap sack, and send me flying down the street. All the hotels would have a man ready to grab the delivery as soon as I got there. We fooled the police for more than a year. In the winter I'd run it down by sleigh."

"And you never got caught?" Fahd asked.

The old man shook his head. "My daddy did, though. He made his own delivery one day when I was at school. Cost him six months."

"Did he pay you for it?" Fahd asked.

The eyes twinkled again.

"Yes, sir, he did indeed."

"What?"

"I got one candy bar for every successful delivery."

Nish looked like he'd just met his soulmate.

6

"I DON'T BELIEVE IT!"

Muck was staring, open-mouthed, over the ice surface at the Park City rink.

The Portland Panthers were playing the Hollywood Stars. The Owls had come to take in the game – scout the opposition, Mr. Dillinger had joked – and they were sitting as a group opposite the two team benches.

The scoreboard had just changed again.

Hollywood Stars 4, Portland Panthers 0.

Travis Lindsay could not believe it either. He could not believe the score, and he could not believe the crowd. All the parents of the Hollywood Stars were sitting together, and all of them wore identical black-and-gold track suits with the sun exploding on the back and the name "Hollywood Stars" emblazoned on the shoulders. On the left arm, where the team players had their names, the parents had "Parent" or "Booster" stitched on.

Travis thought they looked ridiculous.

Dead centre in the parents' area were four very large and burly bodyguards creating a space between Troy Prince and Isabella Val d'Or and the rest of the parents.

Brody Prince's parents were watching the game with their arms around each other. They were both wearing sunglasses.

Sunglasses – in a hockey rink? Not even Nish had thought of that!

"This," Muck said, "is absolutely unbelievable."

The Hollywood Stars had three coaches on the bench, with the head coach wearing a headset and microphone that presumably allowed him to communicate directly with the video coach out in the trailer the Owls had noticed parked alongside the Hollywood Stars' black-and-gold team bus. There were cameras set up about the rink, each one sweeping the action by remote control.

Travis wondered what Brody Prince's parents kept staring down at, until he realized they had a monitor in front of them and that Troy Prince, Brody's father, was also equipped with headphones. Troy Prince was talking into the small microphone. Travis looked at the Stars' bench. The coach was nodding. He changed the players up, sending Brody Prince out on a new line.

"Tell me this isn't happening," Muck said to no one in particular.

So far, the Stars had used the neutral-zone trap to confuse the Panthers, refusing to forecheck and instead waiting until they could squeeze the puck carrier and force a pass that was gobbled up by the remaining four Stars players, who had formed a line at centre. It had worked brilliantly, causing several turnovers and giving the Stars a quick lead on two goals by Brody Prince and two others by his wingers.

But after the Stars had taken their 4-0 lead, the Panthers countered with their own trap, producing some rather dull hockey in which each team simply dumped the puck into the other end, chased it, and hoped for a turnover.

Now, however, the Stars changed strategy.

"They're setting up the 'torpedo'!" Muck roared with laughter.

Travis understood. The trap had become so effective in hockey in recent years that everyone had tried to break it. The best system had come out of Sweden, and Lars, of course, knew all about it. It was called the "torpedo," and it needed four forwards, one as a playmaking centre and one back in the defensive position to fire long breakaway passes to the two torpedoes who simply raced through the other team's trap.

The Stars set up their torpedo, and Brody Prince, who had excellent speed, broke hard over centre, slamming his stick on the ice for a pass. The passer hit him perfectly at the Panthers' blueline, sending Brody Prince on a clear breakaway.

He came in fast, dropped the puck into his skate blades, then chipped it back up quickly onto his stick, fooling the goalie entirely, and flicked the puck into a wide-open side of the net.

"*Hot dog!*" Nish called out.

"*You're one to talk!*" shouted back Sam.

"He's a jerk!" muttered Nish.

"We think he's kind of cute!" giggled Sarah, sitting beside Sam.

The Hollywood Stars' parents were on their feet, cheering wildly. In the centre of the crowd, Troy Prince pumped his fist five times into the air to signal the 5–0 lead.

Travis looked away, then looked back again.

A rubber glove?

The Owls were still talking about the Hollywood Stars back at the hotel when Muck announced bedtime. Even Muck seemed disheartened by what he had seen. If the Hollywood Stars could crush the Panthers 7–1 – Jeremy Billings scoring a late goal for Portland on a solo rush – what would they do to the Owls? The Owls and Panthers, after all, had proved to be almost equal in all the times they had met before.

But it went deeper than that. Muck could handle losing. In fact, he never seemed upset by a loss and always spoke well of the teams that had beaten them. He clearly didn't like what they had seen at the rink that day. Muck – who still wore his old junior gloves and jackets, whose track pants were the subject of endless jokes and even several fundraising attempts by the team to replace them – was repulsed by the *richness* of the Stars, the display of wealth that included the bus, the track suits, the headphones.

And he had thought the tactics being used by the team were hardly in keeping with good hockey. Muck not only despised the trap as being bad for the game, he hated it when coaches had so much control. Hockey, he believed, was about creativity and desire, the team providing the base and the organization, but the players providing the skills. He wished the National Hockey League would give the game back to the players. He did not like to see NHL tactics come down to the peewee level. If the fun was taken out of the game, he wanted nothing to do with it.

The Owls players were similarly unimpressed with the style of play they had seen. But they had to admit there was considerable skill on the Stars' side, particularly when it came to Brody Prince, the team captain and key centre.

Even so, all the boys on the team thought he was a show-off and a jerk.

All the girls thought he was cute.

They were just heading off up to their rooms when Mr. Dillinger came in through the revolving doors, his cheeks flushed from the cold. He seemed in shock.

Muck, already at the elevator, turned and looked at Mr. Dillinger, waiting for him to speak.

Mr. Dillinger seemed at a loss for words. "There's been . . . an incident," he said finally.

"What?" Muck asked.

Mr. Dillinger swallowed. "A player is missing."

"Which team?"

"Hollywood . . . It's the kid, the Prince kid."

"Brody Prince?" Sarah half shrieked.

Mr. Dillinger nodded. "After the game," he said, his words not coming smoothly, "he left the dressing room for the bus and never made it."

"Wasn't anyone with him?"

"He's the only player missing."

"What about his bodyguard?" Fahd asked.

Mr. Dillinger looked stunned.

"He's apparently missing too."

7

THE HEART HAD GONE OUT OF NISH'S GROSS-OUT Olympics.

He tried to hold the third event, The Slurp, but Sarah, who was supposed to be the Owls' competitor in the event, said she *already* felt like throwing up; pulling pantyhose over her head before trying to slurp up a bowl of purple Jell-O would be the same thing as deliberately sticking a finger down her throat.

Nish wisely cancelled the games "until further notice." No one felt like screaming and laughing and acting silly the way they did for the Fly on the Wall and the Snot Shot. It just didn't seem right, under the circumstances.

The circumstances were these: Brody Prince was missing and presumed kidnapped. The bodyguard was missing and presumed to be part of the kidnap plot. Beyond that, little was known.

Data, of course, had all the latest news. When he wasn't sitting around the hotel lobby waiting for the latest edition of the *Salt Lake City Star* to be delivered to the lobby gift shop, he was surfing the Internet for all the Web sites, from CNN to

USA Today. None of them, however, had as much detailed coverage as the local daily:

ROCK CHILD MISSING
AND PRESUMED KIDNAPPED

By Randolph J. Saxon, Star Staff

The child of entertainment superstar Troy Prince, missing since Wednesday evening, is now presumed to have been kidnapped and held for ransom, Utah State Police have confirmed.

The Federal Bureau of Investigation has been called in to take over the case of 13-year-old Brody Prince's mysterious disappearance.

The young son of the rock and movie mogul and Isabella Val d'Or, the former supermodel, went missing following a hockey game in the Peewee Olympics currently under way at venues in Salt Lake City, Ogden, and Park City.

Following a match between Prince's Hollywood Stars and the Portland Panthers held Wednesday in Park City, Troy Prince disappeared from the hotel where the Hollywood team, which is heavily financed by his parents, was staying.

Also missing is Taras Zimbalist, 32, a bodyguard hired last summer by the Prince family specifically to watch over their only child.

A police source has told the *Star* that Zimbalist is presumed by the FBI to be part of the kidnap plot, though the FBI has refused all comment on the case.

Troy Prince, known for his eccentricities as well as his hits, was estimated by *Fortune* magazine earlier this spring to be worth in excess of $2 billion.

Less than a day later, the paper had advanced the story considerably, leaving no doubt as to the motive behind the disappearance.

KIDNAP VICTIM PRESUMED
SPIRITED OUT OF STATE

By Randolph J. Saxon, Star Staff

Brody Prince, the 13-year-old child of entertainment superstar Troy Prince, was flown out of Utah following his kidnapping, according to police sources.

The *Star* has learned that kidnappers had an intricate plan in place following Wednesday's abduction of the young hockey player in Park City.

Primary suspect Taras Zimbalist, 32, the boy's bodyguard, is also said to have left the state via the same route, leading police to speculate that the kidnapping was planned by experts and carried out by several persons, including Zimbalist.

Witnesses have apparently told police they sighted a long black limousine hurrying from the Park City arena site shortly after the game ended between the Hollywood Stars and the Portland Panthers.

Both teams were competing in the Peewee Olympics and Prince failed to make the Hollywood team bus following his team's victory over the Portland squad.

According to *Star* sources, the limousine was seen traveling at speeds in excess of 100 mph on the route out to the county airport on the outskirts of Park City.

One witness, police say, reported sounds of a large helicopter taking off at around the time the limousine would have reached the small airfield.

Police checks of other Utah airports suggest no mysterious helicopter landings that night, leading police to presume the helicopter headed for Nevada, perhaps Las Vegas.

The investigation is now shifting to other states.

No ransom note has been received so far, police sources say.

The Prince family has made no public comment since the boy went missing.

The speculation was wild. The Mob was involved, one commentator said on CNN. One man being interviewed went so far as to suggest that the boy had engineered his own disappearance to get away from his mad father.

Background checks of Zimbalist found that he was working with false identification and references, and was, in fact, Lawrence "Big Larry" Prado, who had previously served time in federal prison for counterfeiting and assault.

The world media was flooding into Park City, taking up the few remaining empty hotel rooms and bringing huge satellite trucks up into the mountains to report live on location about the case.

The arrival of the satellite trucks and the television cameras brought Troy Prince and Isabella Val d'Or out of the seclusion of their luxury hotel. They appeared on the front steps of the Park City police station before a swarm of television cameras and microphones, and Troy Prince made an impassioned plea to the kidnappers to let his son go.

The Owls all gathered around the television set in the lobby of their own hotel to watch and listen. As Troy Prince spoke, tears rolled down his cheeks.

"He's heartbroken!" Sarah all but wailed as she watched, tears forming in her own eyes.

"C'mon," said Nish with even more than his usual sarcasm. "You forget he's an actor – he can cry at the drop of a hat."

Sam threw one of the sofa cushions at him. "You're *pathetic!*" she shouted as he scuttled away.

"I was just saying he's an actor . . . ," Nish protested weakly, the colour rising in his cheeks.

"And the whole thing's fake?" Sam countered. "I don't think so. Brody Prince could be lying dead somewhere for all we know."

Travis said nothing, but he didn't think so. No one would want to kill a thirteen-year-old peewee hockey player, no matter how rude he could be or how much better he thought he was than everyone else. But they might want to kidnap him and hold him for ransom. Travis figured Brody Prince was, at this very moment, being held in some well-guarded hotel room in Las Vegas, his captors watching this very same broadcast as they decided how much to ask for and when to ask for it.

Travis wondered how much it would be.

A million?

Ten million?

A *billion* dollars?

He wondered how much his parents would pay to get him back if someone ever kidnapped the captain of the Screech Owls of little Tamarack.

A hundred dollars?

Two hundred?

He wondered how much Nish's poor mom would give up to get back her little trouble-making darling. Travis giggled to himself.

A loonie?

He was instantly ashamed of himself. This was no laughing matter. Even if he didn't like Brody Prince, he didn't want anything to happen to him. He didn't even want to play the Stars – if it came to that – without Brody Prince, even if he was by far their top player.

Travis wanted him back, and in the lineup – and then he wouldn't feel so badly about wanting the insufferable Brody Prince to lose.

8

NISH SEEMED DEPRESSED. HE'D GIVEN UP, AT least temporarily, on the Gross-Out Olympics, and was no longer saying a word about what he planned to bury at centre ice for the gold-medal game at the E Center in Salt Lake City. Nish was, for the first time in his life, quiet and well-mannered and keeping very much to himself. He was even reading a book.

If Travis hadn't known better, he'd have suggested to Mr. Dillinger that perhaps Nish needed medical attention.

All the Owls were down. Sam and Sarah kept bursting into tears whenever they were together and someone started talking about the kidnapping. And not just the Owls, but the other players on other teams seemed to have lost their appetite for what should have been a once-in-a-lifetime experience. Travis had run into Jeremy Billings at the third-floor pop machine and Jeremy said it was the same with the Panthers: everyone was down, everyone had lost heart in the tournament.

But the games would go on, the organizers insisted. The *real* Olympics had, over the years, continued through terrorist attack, a bomb, political and financial scandals, and the Peewee Olympics deserved no less.

Troy Prince released a statement in which the family insisted the tournament should continue, and the Hollywood Stars voted to stay on even without their best player.

It all made sense to Travis. What else was there to do? Quitting the tournament wasn't going to force the kidnappers to hand back Brody Prince. Everyone going home wouldn't mean that the kidnapping had never happened. The best the teams could do was to stay put and wait and see what happened next. Would the kidnappers demand a ransom? Or would the police catch the kidnappers?

And what would happen to Brody Prince in all of this, Travis wondered. No one thought the young player had been hurt, but there was the distinct possibility that this could still happen. If the police were closing in, the kidnappers might panic. If the Prince family refused to pay, the kidnappers might take revenge.

Travis tried to imagine how Brody would be feeling. Was he scared? Would he believe his father would pay the ransom? Would he want the police to find out where he was or would he hope they never came close to the kidnappers?

And where was he? In a Las Vegas hotel? In a

cabin high in the mountains? In another country? Was he tied up? Was he being held at gunpoint? Was he being fed and cared for?

Was he scared?

It always came back to that. Of course he would be scared, Travis decided. How could he not be?

Two days after Brody Prince went missing the Owls played the Long Island Selects – winning handily on Sarah's hat trick and some outstanding goaltending by Jeremy Weathers – and when they came back to the hotel there was a report on CNN that the kidnappers had finally made contact. The ransom they demanded, according to the television network, was several million dollars.

"Pocket change," Nish grumbled as he leaned his chin on his fists, carefully watching the report from Salt Lake City.

"Will they pay it?" Fahd asked.

"Of course they will," Sam said. "It's nothing to a man like Troy Prince."

"But *should* they pay?" Lars asked. "It's only an encouragement to other kidnappers, isn't it?"

Lars had a point, and the Owls began a long and spirited discussion on kidnapping and ransoms and whether you should give in to criminals like that. The alternative, however, was to endanger the kidnapped person and risk never getting that person back safely.

It was a difficult question, and no one could come up with a satisfactory answer – the Owls just knew that they all wished Brody Prince would return safely, and soon.

They were talking this way – Nish and Sam getting louder and louder – when Data suddenly brought the room to a halt by raising his good arm and loudly demanding they all "shush."

There was an item on CNN, another report from Salt Lake City. A body had been found outside a municipal dump near the far end of the Great Salt Lake flats.

Murder was uncommon enough in this state, and particularly unnerving was that it had happened the same week as the kidnapping.

The normally quiet Salt Lake City was suddenly looking like the crime capital of North America.

The body had been found by city workers doing a general cleanup of an old gravel pit. So far it had not been identified and police had said there appeared to be "no connection between the discovery of the body and the recent kidnapping of Brody Prince, son of wealthy entertainer Troy Prince."

The body, according to police, belonged to an elderly man who had died under "uncertain circumstances." Foul play was suspected, but police so far had no idea how the man had been killed or why his body had been dumped there.

CNN had obtained a police artist's sketch of the elderly victim and the screen suddenly filled with a roughly drawn portrait.

It was of a very old man. He had long white hair and a very long waxed moustache. All that was missing was the twinkle in his eye.

"*Ebenezer!*" Nish shouted.

No one else had to say a word. They had all recognized the portrait.

It was, without question, Ebenezer Durk.

9

THE OWLS SLEPT BADLY THAT NIGHT. TRAVIS ached from a shot he'd taken in the leg when one of the Selects forwards had tipped a point shot from Sam, but it wasn't that sort of hurt that kept him tossing and turning long into the dark hours. It was a different sort of hurt, almost as if he'd taken the puck in his gut rather than in his calf. A few times, as Travis lay staring out the hotel window into the blue glow of the night sky, he was certain he heard Nish sobbing, but he said nothing, deciding to let Nish deal with his own pain in his own way.

Their new friend Ebenezer Durk was dead.

Mr. Dillinger had immediately phoned the police to offer an identification, but by the time his call got through the authorities had already received dozens of others from people in Park City who had recognized Ebenezer's striking moustache in the artist's sketch.

In the morning, the papers were filled with stories about the discovery, as well as with new information on the ransom demand.

NABBERS WANT $10 MILLION

By Randolph J. Saxon, Star Staff

The kidnappers of Brody Prince have made contact with the Prince family, police sources confirmed late last evening following an underworld tip received by the *Star*.

According to the *Star* tipster, the amount sought is $10 million. Neither the police nor a spokesperson for wealthy entertainer Troy Prince, father of the missing peewee hockey player Brody Prince, would confirm the figure.

Police will say, however, that an e-mail was received at Prince Entertainment headquarters in Hollywood that appears genuine. Whoever wrote the message provided key information that indicated they were indeed connected to Wednesday's kidnapping following a peewee tournament game in Park City.

Sources have further told the *Star* that the money is to be delivered to a secret site in Nevada, adding to speculation that young Prince was immediately whisked from Utah to the neighboring state by helicopter.

Police are concentrating search efforts in the Las Vegas and Reno areas, with suspicion mounting that the intricately planned kidnapping might be connected to organized crime.

The accounts of the body were somewhat vague – the stories hinting that police knew who it was but had yet to confirm the identity of the dead man – and confusing. One account said the victim had been shot, another had him being stabbed. Police, the newspaper said, were to drag the nearby shoreline of Salt Lake that day in search of the murder weapon.

Late in the afternoon, the media had the name of the murdered man, confirmed through dental records as Ebenezer Durk, and the radio and television broadcasts were already filling with speculation as to why anyone would want to kill a gentle old man who worked part-time as a volunteer giving tours in Park City.

According to one rumour, Ebenezer Durk was a holder of vast wealth, inherited from his bootlegger father who had apparently made a fortune during Prohibition days when alcohol was illegal throughout the west. The money was believed to be buried in Durk's yard or simply hidden under his mattress.

One report, however, said there had been no sign of an intruder at Durk's humble little home just outside Park City. Nor had neighbours seen Durk with anyone lately. Apart from his volunteer work, he went out very little.

The most intriguing report was on the six o'clock news, when the CBS affiliate reporter, standing in front of the morgue, announced that not only had the police been unsuccessful in their search for a murder weapon, the chief coroner's office did not even know what they were looking for.

"Sources tell CBS News," the reporter said, "that the elderly man was killed with a weapon so far unknown to criminal investigators. Both a gun and a knife have been ruled out by forensic experts, and the investigation now centres on what it was that fatally pierced the heart of Ebenezer Durk."

"*What the . . .?*" said Nish, who was near tears.

"Some experts!" said Andy. "They don't have a clue!"

"All they have to do is find the weapon," said Fahd, "and then they'll know."

Data, who had been sitting in his wheelchair saying nothing, suddenly hit the remote control to turn off the television. Everyone turned at once to him, wondering what on earth he was doing.

Data seemed nervous, frightened. He swallowed hard.

The others all waited, almost afraid to breathe.

Finally, Data spoke. "They won't ever find the weapon."

A look of incredulity came over each and every face in the lobby – Data's excepted.

"What do you mean 'won't ever *find* the weapon'?" Sarah asked.

"Because it doesn't exist," Data said.

"*Doesn't exist?*" Sam all but shouted. "What the heck does *that* mean?"

"It doesn't exist," Data insisted.

"How do you know?" asked Travis.

"Because," Data said carefully, "I think I know what killed Ebenezer Durk."

10

THE OWLS GATHERED IN DATA'S ROOM AND waited patiently while he and Fahd hooked the laptop up to Data's digital camera.

Data used the mouse to race through the photographs he had taken since the team left Tamarack for the long bus ride to Salt Lake City: shots of the players sleeping, shots of various sites along the way, a great photo of Nish sound asleep with a sagging top hat of shaving cream on his head, shots of their arrival, the mountains, the hotel, the rinks, and then photos of the tour of Park City the Owls had taken with Ebenezer Durk.

Travis waited patiently as Data flicked through the shots of the old buildings and the small underground jail, then began racing through a series of photographs of the snowfall and the walk around to the stables behind Main Street.

Data stopped, backed up, and settled on a photo of the stables with the icicles hanging from their eaves reaching nearly to the ground. Travis shivered just remembering that astonishingly cold day.

Data used the mouse to zoom in on the icicles, the long swords of ice glistening deep blue in the sun.

It was a lovely photo, a postcard.

"There's your murder weapon," Data said.

"Where?" Nish asked.

"Right in front of your eyes."

"He was killed with a *laptop*?" Nish said, his eyes widening.

Data sighed deeply. Fahd giggled and then bit back the giggle.

"The perfect murder weapon," Data said. "An icicle. The only murder weapon known that is guaranteed to melt away and never be seen again."

Travis held his tongue in the turmoil that followed. The Owls excitedly talked about how ingenious it was to use an icicle to stab someone. The murder weapon could be laid right on top of the body and by the time the police arrived it would have turned into a puddle from the warmth of the body alone. A little longer under the right conditions, and the murder weapon might vanish entirely – evaporated into thin air.

"Brilliant," Jesse said.

"But wouldn't it break?" asked Liz.

"Not if the stab was straight on," said Data.

"An icicle would work if it was long enough and thick enough."

These icicles were both long enough and thick. Fahd kept zooming in and out on them, his teammates leaning behind him now and shivering – even though the room was perfectly warm.

"They found his body by the lake, though," said Simon. "The storm didn't hit there, did it? Wasn't it just here, in the mountains?"

"I think he was killed right here and taken to that gravel pit," said Data. "That way the police would never figure out how they'd killed him."

"But . . . ," said Sam, her pause capturing the attention of all the Owls, "but if that's what happened . . . who killed him?"

"That's the next part of the mystery," said Data, "and we don't have a cluc."

Travis cleared his throat. He knew he was blushing, almost afraid to say what he knew had to be said.

"Maybe . . . ," he began, waiting while the others turned to listen, "maybe we do have a clue."

11

WITH THE REST OF THE TEAM HANGING ON HIS every word, Travis told the tale of wandering away from the stable doors and bumping into the two men, at least one of them a bodyguard he'd recognized from the fancy hotel lobby when the Prince family had first arrived in Park City.

"Why didn't you say anything?" Derek asked.

"I just thought they'd taken a wrong turn or something. Maybe they had."

"I doubt it," said Data, who more and more was taking control of the investigation. "I think they were there looking for Ebenezer and didn't expect us to be there."

"But why?" asked Jenny.

Data considered a moment. "If they came looking for him, he must have had something they wanted, or needed. And it's just a guess that he was killed by them with one of these icicles — but what else could it be?"

"The question still is why?" said Dmitri. "I can't follow it at all."

"Well," said Data, "consider this: they came

for a reason, they didn't expect to find us there, and they came back later. Then, for some reason or other, they killed Ebenezer and took his body off to that gravel pit."

"Why would they do that?" asked Andy.

"Presumably," said Data, "so no one would connect the murder to the location."

"I think they wanted to know about the tunnels," Travis said suddenly.

Everyone turned, listening.

"They needed Ebenezer to explain how the tunnels worked," Travis continued. "He knew everything about them. Those two must have been involved with the bodyguard in the kidnapping. Maybe they wanted to sneak up on Brody Prince using the tunnels. And when Ebenezer wouldn't tell them, they got mad and killed him."

All around, the Owls were nodding. All except Nish.

Nish was red-faced, close to tears. "Or maybe he did tell them," Nish said, "and they killed him anyway."

Several of the Owls turned fast on Nish, their faces filled with confusion.

"That makes no sense," said Sam.

"It does," argued Nish, "if they wanted to keep using the tunnels."

Everyone considered that possibility for a moment. It was so unlike Nish to come up with any insight, to think of something possible – not something bordering on the insane – that no one else had considered.

And yet . . .

"But that would mean they never left Utah with Brody," Data finally said.

"Exactly," said Nish.

"But there are witnesses," Fahd countered, shaking his head at Nish's failure to remember the reports of the limo and later the helicopter.

"Maybe the witnesses were part of the plan," said Nish.

"*What?*" Fahd howled. "'Fake' witnesses – give me a break!"

"No," countered Nish. "I'm saying there *was* a limo and even a helicopter – but maybe they were diversionary tactics."

"Where are you getting this from?" demanded Fahd. "The *movies*?"

"Well," said Nish, beginning to enjoy the fact that he now had the attention of every Owl in the room, "think about it. They set up the limo and the chopper and instantly everyone thinks that Brody has been whisked away and the police start looking for him in another state – when all along he's right below us!"

For a long time, no one said a word. Then, dramatically, Data snapped down the lid of his laptop and turned to the red-faced Nish.

"I never thought I'd say this as long as I lived," he began.

"What?" Nish asked quickly, worried about what might be coming.

"Nish – you're a *genius*!"

12

THE SALT LAKE CITY POLICE GAVE THE SCREECH Owls short shrift when they heard the team's ideas on what might have happened to Ebenezer Durk. Mr. Dillinger had offered to make the phone call – it being fairly obvious that the police would pay more attention to a responsible adult than to a twelve-year-old defenceman with a ridiculous name like Nish – but even Mr. Dillinger seemed to carry little weight with the police. They listened to the theory about the icicles and said it was highly unlikely, but nothing had been ruled out yet and forensic tests were continuing. They dismissed outright the theory that Brody Prince was being held in the tunnels and caverns underneath the Main Street of Park City, saying the area had been searched carefully at least three times and police were satisfied with the eye-witness accounts of the dark limousine's run out to the little airport to meet the helicopter.

Mr. Dillinger seemed deeply discouraged by the response, and sagged visibly at the end of his brief talk with the police community-relations officer.

"They're not much interested in what we think," he told the Owls, who had assembled to listen in on the conversation they had believed would, as Derek put it, "blow the case wide open."

"They're making a big mistake," said Data, who seemed particularly hurt by the response.

Mr. Dillinger picked himself up and shook his head. "Well, we can't dwell on it. At least we've told them what we think – now let's get organized. *We have a hockey game to play!*"

Mr. Dillinger's words were like a splash of cold water in the face for the Owls, most of whom had all but forgotten about the tournament.

Travis checked his watch. Less than two hours to get to the rink and get ready – *really* ready.

The Owls were about to play the dreaded Toronto Towers, the team that had beaten them in overtime to win the Little Stanley Cup tournament a few months earlier.

Win this match, however, and the Screech Owls were guaranteed a place in the medal round.

Lose, and there was no chance at all of any medal – let alone the cherished gold.

"We're here to play hockey," Muck told the Owls as they were getting dressed for the game. "We have to remember that. All the stuff that happens away from the rink – no matter how bad it is –

has nothing to do with the game we play as a team, understand?"

Several of the Owls nodded. Travis pulled his jersey over his head, making sure to kiss it just as the captain's "C" slid by.

"You can let yourselves dwell on what has happened, have no focus, and if we lose we'll head back home," Muck continued. "Or you can win one for Mr. Durk, in his memory, and make sure we stick around to watch out for him – because no one else seems to be doing it."

With that, Muck turned abruptly and left the room, shutting the door quietly behind him.

No one said a word.

All Travis could hear was the sound of Mr. Dillinger polishing the skate-sharpening machine as he very lightly whistled.

"How many words in the Gettysburg Address?" Gordie Griffith suddenly asked the assembled Screech Owls.

Only one of them, however, would know. "Two hundred and seventy-two," Willie Granger, the Owls' trivia expert, immediately answered.

"How many in what Muck just said to us?" Gordie asked.

Willie shrugged. "I dunno – a *hundred*?"

"Well, it adds up to just as much," Gordie said, and began banging his stick on the cement floor.

The other Owls grabbed their sticks and began pounding on the floor as well, a rising drumbeat of support for poor Ebenezer Durk, who, as Muck had just said, had no one else to look out for him, and for the Screech Owls of Tamarack – hockey team extraordinaire.

"They should be checking birth certificates," Nish mumbled to Travis after the warm-up.

Travis nodded. The Towers seemed even bigger, if anything, than they had back in Toronto when they'd beaten the Owls in the championship game. All of them except the slim girl who'd been the Towers' entrant in the Fly on the Wall event literally towered over the Owls, with only Andy Higgins, Samantha, and Nish looking as if they'd fit on the Toronto team, the rest of the Owls either too small, too short, or too slight even to belong on the same ice surface as this hulking group of skaters.

But the Owls had size of a different kind. They had hearts so big it evened out the differences in body size the moment the puck was dropped.

Sarah won the opening faceoff and dropped a backhand through her legs to Nish, moving up fast, and Nish immediately whipped a backhand pass over to Dmitri, who'd circled back of his right wing.

The Towers, caught flatfooted, seemed to lose composure instantly. One defenceman lunged to catch Dmitri, who proved far too quick on his turn, thereby trapping the defender in the wrong zone as the Owls broke over the Towers' blueline four abreast, with Nish joining the rush.

Dmitri flipped a high pass that floated right across to Travis and landed at his feet. Travis kicked the puck ahead onto his stick blade and dug hard for the corner.

Nish read Travis perfectly. The Toronto players figured Travis would scoot behind the net and try the wraparound as he looped to the other side, but Nish and Travis had practised the reversal so often it was second nature for Nish to sprint to the opposite side of the net as everyone else focused on where they expected the puck to end up.

Travis played it just right. With the goaltender already drifting across the crease to cut off the wraparound, Travis dropped a quick pass from behind the net back to the corner he had just rounded – with Nish cutting fast across the ice to slap it home into an empty side.

The Owls had drawn first blood.

The Towers never recovered from that opening faceoff. Sarah scored a second goal on a brilliant rush where she split the defence, Dmitri scored one of his patented flying-water-bottle goals, and Travis scored on a deflection to give the first line a goal each.

The Towers scored only once in the first period and once in the second, but then little Simon

Milliken, from his knees, chipped a puck in under the Toronto crossbar to make it 5–2.

Late in the third period, with the Towers failing to draw the Owls into penalties and growing ever more discouraged, Travis picked up a puck in his own end and broke hard up his wing. He looked back to see what was assembling on the ice: Sarah clear at centre, Dmitri breaking, Nish hustling to join the rush.

Travis hit Dmitri with a long pass and Dmitri jumped around the defence as if the other player were tied to a kitchen chair. Instead of cutting for the net, however, Dmitri turned sharply towards the boards, circling back and putting a perfect pass on Sarah's stick as she came across the blueline.

Travis raised his stick for the shot. He saw Nish out of the corner of his eye, moving hard towards the net on the far side.

Sarah passed perfectly.

Travis swung his stick at the puck – deliberately missing it! He heard the quick bark of a laugh from the Towers' bench – a player or coach thinking Travis had fanned on the shot.

The puck went through his legs and straight to Nish, who was also ready. He hammered the puck with all his strength, the puck flying hard off his stick, up over the shoulder of the Towers' goaltender.

And off the post!

It didn't matter. The game was soon over, the Owls were the winners, and they were headed for the championship round.

"*Perfect!*" a sweating, red-faced Nish shouted as he clicked helmets with Travis.

"We missed!" Travis giggled, not caring.

"We won't next time."

13

TRAVIS MISSED THE ICE THE MOMENT HE STEPPED off it.

Sometimes the game seemed to him like another world, another dimension, where life was protected from everything else. There was no homework in a hockey game, no garbage to carry out, no lawn to cut, no crime – apart from tripping and interference – and most assuredly no murder.

On the ice, time was frozen. Off the ice, it seemed speeded up. Reporters from around the world were still staking out the Prince family, and the news was filled with stories of kidnapping and murder. The television news said that forensic scientists working on the murder of Ebenezer Durk had ruled out a knife and were looking for some other form of very sharp object, perhaps plastic, perhaps wooden – not even a mention of ice.

The newspaper said that police in Reno had raided a hotel room where it was believed Brody Prince was being held by his captors, but the raid had produced nothing except some scribbled notes that police would not comment on. No one but the Owls seemed to think for a moment that the young peewee player might still be in Utah.

The teams tried to keep their minds on the tournament. Nish continued to suspend his Gross-Out Olympics, but there were still the scheduled activities and a lot of free time available for the Owls to do other things.

When most of the Owls headed off for a morning of skiing and snowboarding on the mountains surrounding the town, Sarah suggested to Travis that they try the toboggan run behind the hotel – and that they invite Nish along for a specific reason.

"We'll need the weight," she said, giggling.

Nish, of course, was keen to try anything with even a hint of danger in it.

The toboggan run had been made by hotel workers with banked-up, ice-covered snow. It reminded Travis of the track he once received at Christmas and set up on the basement stairs to shoot tiny metal cars from one side of the basement to the other. They generally crashed into the far wall and, as intended, burst into numerous parts that could then be put back together.

The toboggan run at full speed was no game, though, and Travis was quickly convinced, as the sled flew down the groomed and iced run, that if they ever hit a wall at this speed they would indeed burst into parts – never to be put back together again.

He was frightened and thrilled at the same time, grateful to be wearing a crash helmet in case they somehow flew off the track. Nish loved it, screaming as the wind cut into their faces and even volunteering to lug the heavy toboggan back up for a second and a third run.

Travis was happy that Sarah, not Nish, was steering. Sarah kept cool and calm, guiding the hurtling vehicle perfectly in and out of the corners, never once flying free of the run.

In the evening they all gathered again in the lobby while Muck and Mr. Dillinger met with tournament officials in preparation for the finals.

Data and Fahd had been busy. When Fahd pushed Data into the lobby, he was carrying two large battery-powered lanterns on his lap.

"What's *that* all about?" Sam wanted to know.

Data picked one of the lanterns up and turned it on, the flash spreading across the darkened lobby.

"It's time for the Owls to go underground."

14

TRAVIS HAD THAT FAMILIAR UNEASY FEELING.

He hated enclosed spaces. He hated the dark and still slept with a night light whenever he could. But now he was headed down into the narrow pitch–black tunnel beneath Park City, with nothing but a single lantern and a desperate urge to grab Sarah's sleeve and hold on for dear life.

Data had assigned the tunnels higher up to Travis, Sarah, Dmitri, and Nish. Fahd, Andy, Sam, and Simon would take the lower tunnels.

Data, with the help of Willie's amazing memory, had mapped out all the twists and turns Ebenezer Durk had shown them. He had also used his laptop to get into the town archives and had linked to a state-university paper on the rum-running scheme that included maps of the original tunnel structure. Data had then used his laptop to overlay the tunnels on a current chamber-of-commerce map of the downtown, and each team now had a printout of where the tunnels ran and their relation to the streets above.

Data had come to the conclusion that the police could not possibly have searched all the tunnels. The investigators said they had checked all the passageways, but Data's research showed numerous branches that were now blocked off from the main tunnels. There seemed to be no direct route to the series of tunnels Ebenezer Durk had shown the Owls, and Data insisted that the police would not have checked Ebenezer Durk's secret passages beneath the old stable.

Travis was impressed, but he was also desperate to get out of these dark, dank caves as quickly as possible.

Sarah led the way with the lantern, heading along a corridor below the stables that ran, according to Data's map, up Main Street towards an old hotel.

It was tough going. Some of the passages were blocked off, some seemed to have caved in. The tunnel they were following was the one Ebenezer Durk had shown them, and, thankfully, it had been buttressed with beams and wooden planking.

Travis could hear water dripping, which made him puzzle over how water could run down here when all was frozen above. He thought, too, that he heard something scurrying.

Rats?

He decided to say nothing to Sarah; the last thing he wanted was for her to panic. If she was frightened, she was not showing it, moving ahead carefully in a crouch, seemingly ready to react to whatever might be around the next turn.

But around the next turn there was only more darkness, and more turns to come. More darkness. More blockages. More dead ends.

"This is useless," Nish grumbled from behind. "There's no one here."

"We have to check everything out," Travis whispered. "You never know."

But Travis, too, was losing heart. In a way, he was grateful for the growing sense that there was nothing down here but a musty smell, pitch black, and the odd rat. But in another way he was disappointed they hadn't found anything to support Nish's surprise theory that the kidnappers had faked their own escape and were still in Park City.

Travis was beginning to doubt it.

He wasn't even thinking of the possibilities when, in the poor light, he walked into Sarah's back.

She had stopped fast.

Nish stepped into Travis.

"*What — ?*"

"Shhhhhhh," Sarah hissed.

Simon crouched down low and ducked under Nish's arm to move into the front, but Sarah reached back and caught him by the collar.

Travis leaned out around Sarah to stare down the narrow tunnel.

At first he saw nothing. Then, slowly, a pinprick of light became visible in the distance.

It couldn't be Sam and the others – they had gone in the other direction.

They had no choice but to try to get closer.

15

MAYBE WE SHOULD GO BACK," NISH SAID IN A whisper that shook.

"It might be our only chance," said Sarah. She swiftly killed the light and pressed on.

They moved in silence, their feet sure along the rock paths, their hands out to one side so they could run their fingers along the shored-up walls.

As their eyes adjusted to the darkness, the light in the distance slowly took on a new brilliance. Travis could see that it was steady, not moving, and presumed it was either a bulb or an electric lantern someone had hung up on a wall. He could detect no movement around it and was grateful for that.

They drew closer, increasingly afraid of stumbling or even breathing too hard.

Sarah held her hand back, touching Travis, then Nish, indicating that they should stop. She whispered so low they could hardly hear her. "I'll go on my own from here."

She handed Travis the lantern. There was no arguing with her. It was too risky to talk, for one thing. But neither was there any point: she had her mind made up.

Travis felt helpless as Sarah disappeared into the near-total darkness. A few times she cast a long shadow as she moved quickly up the tunnel and was caught by the distant light, but most of the time he could detect nothing. She moved in complete silence.

Travis tried to control his breathing. He could hear Nish breathing hard beside him and once or twice Simon stifled a cough. But none of them said a thing.

Travis squinted hard, trying to force his eyes to see more clearly.

There was more movement nearer the light now. The light blacked out entirely as Sarah moved from one side of the tunnel to the other.

Then Travis heard her fall.

Sarah never said a word, but it was clear she'd skidded on loose gravel or a board and had gone down hard.

"*HEY!*" a voice boomed from far off, the sound seeming to grow as it hurled down the tunnel.

None of the Owls said a word.

"*Who's there? What's going on?*"

The voice sounded frantic.

And then came the most terrifying sound Travis Lindsay had ever heard.

KAAAAAAA-BOOOOOOOOOMMMM!

16

IN THE TUNNEL, THE GUNSHOT SOUNDED LIKE A cannon going off inside Travis's ear.

Nish hit the ground beside him and Simon screamed.

Travis heard Sarah scrambling back towards them.

Thank heaven – she hadn't been hit!

The tunnel, so silent a moment ago he could hear water drip, now thundered with sound: the echoing gunshot, Sarah stumbling as she ran back to them, Nish grunting as he got to his feet again, the shouts that came from the far pinpoint of light where the gunshot had come from. There had not, mercifully, been a second shot.

Travis knew he would have to show his mettle. He was captain, after all, and Sarah had already upstaged him by advancing alone and unprotected towards the light. He *had* to do something.

There were lights moving now, the dance and skip of flashlight beams coming on and sweeping frantically for the intruder.

Travis felt around on the tunnel floor until he found a rock. He picked it up and tossed it as far as he could up the tunnel, past the dark, crouching, running shadow that he knew to be Sarah. He hoped it would serve as a distraction and confuse them as to which way she had run.

The rock made a lot of noise, but its echo was instantly crushed by a much louder sound.

KAAAAAAA-BOOOOOOOOOOMMMM!

A second shot, echoing down the tunnels.

"*Run for it!*" Sarah gasped as she came into sight.

Simon and Nish were already scrambling to get away. Travis grabbed the lantern from Sarah and pushed her on past him, shoving her hard to make sure she joined them. Sarah paused momentarily, then darted to join the others.

Travis flicked on the light. He knew it was dangerous, perhaps even foolhardy, but he had to get his bearings, had to know what he was dealing with.

There was an old, rotting sawhorse to the side, with boards leaning on it. Likely it had been left over from the last efforts at shoring up the old walls of the tunnels. He flicked off the light immediately and went to work, feeling in the dark as he grabbed the sawhorse and whipped it around to block the tunnel at waist height. The boards he scattered about the barrier at random.

Then, with the light still off, he turned and bolted into the pitch dark after his friends.

Travis had no idea where the turns were. He smacked a shoulder into the rough wall, then ricocheted over to the other side and scraped his cheek. He felt dizzy, felt his knees buckle, but knew he could not go down.

There was light flickering in the tunnel behind him. It bounced wildly along the dark walls. One moment, he was sure he'd be seen, the next he was sure his pursuers – there seemed to be two of them – had no idea where they were heading. He could hear them cursing and grunting, their voices magnified as if through loudspeakers down the narrow tunnel.

Travis used a brief sweep of light to dart farther ahead towards the others. He could see Sarah's white face – terrified – looking back for him.

"*Uhhhhhhhnnnnnnn!*"

"*Owwwwww! What the hell!*"

The cursing was accompanied by a clattering of heavy boards as the two chasers hit Travis's barricade. It had been too low and too dark for them to see it as they scrambled after the intruders. They had hit it full-force.

One flashlight went out – broken, Travis hoped, in the fall. He had no time to find out. He hurried on, quickly switching on and off his light as he rounded turns in the tunnels and caught up to the other three.

KAAAAAAA-BOOOOOOOOOMMMM!

A third shot echoed, but seemed more distant,

less terrifying. It seemed, in fact, to come from another tunnel, and Travis hoped the pursuers had taken a wrong turn after their fall.

He switched his light on.

"Hurry, Trav!" Sarah gasped. "They're coming!"

With the lantern lighting the way, they raced through the tunnels as if they were on wheels and the tunnel were a downhill track, their legs burning as they never did in a hockey game. Nish, who hated having to walk, who once said he wished he could *drive* from his living room to the refrigerator, was flying out in front, with Simon right behind him and Sarah and Travis bringing up the rear.

There were no more gunshots.

Three more turns and Travis could make out the faint light that came from the stables. There was a ladder there, and if they reached it in time, they'd soon be out and onto Main Street.

Nish was already up the ladder when Travis and Sarah reached it. Sarah pushed Simon up by his rear end and then she scrambled up and away.

Travis took one look back – nothing, no sound, not even a flicker of light – and drew a deep breath before climbing up and out.

They broke into the light streaming into the stables, instantly blinded by the forgotten brightness of the day.

It took several seconds for their eyes to adjust, and by the time they had there were sounds of people moving coming from the foot of the ladder.

17

TRAVIS'S PANIC LASTED ONLY A MOMENT – AS long as it took for Sam's head to pop up from below.

It was the second group of Screech Owls.

"What was that sound?" Sam said as the second group climbed out, blinking and squinting into the intense light.

"Sounded like thunder," said Andy. "Or an explosion."

"It was gunshots!" Nish hissed, his face steaming red. "They were *shooting* at us!"

The second group stopped, eyes open wide despite the glare.

"You joke?" said Sam.

Nish shook his head.

"No joke," said Sarah. "They were shooting."

"Who was?" Andy asked.

"We couldn't see them," said Simon, "but it must have been the kidnappers – tourists don't suddenly start shooting while they're on a tour."

"How'd you get away?"

Nish looked up, his face glowing. "I led the way."

Travis glanced at Sarah, who was already rolling her eyes.

"We'd better get the police," said Simon.

"There's no time!" said Sarah. "*Look!*" She was pointing up the alley, the finger of her glove shaking.

A large black car was sliding to a halt on the greasy snow. Then out of the back door of a rundown old building came several men in dark coats and hats.

It was impossible to recognize any of them at this distance, but Travis saw at once that surrounded by the group of men was a smaller body with a black tuque pulled tight over its head.

Brody Prince?

"*They're making a run for it!*" shouted Simon.

The burly men shoved the smaller figure into the back seat of the vehicle, and the big dark car fishtailed wildly as the driver floored the gas pedal and the rear wheels spun helplessly in the slush of the back alley.

The car fishtailed again, bounced off an old delivery truck parked nearby, and spun off onto a side street, heading down from the mountain towards the interstate.

"*They're going to get away!*" screamed Sam. "*And they've got Brody with them!*"

"Not if we can help it!" shouted Sarah. "Nish . . . Trav – follow me!"

Sarah began sprinting through the snow towards Main Street and the Screech Owls' hotel.

She must be racing to get Muck, Travis thought, and ran to catch up, unsure what else to do. Nish hurried along behind them, panting heavily as he ran through deep snow that had drifted against the side of the stables.

But Sarah had no intention of going into the team hotel. She flew down a side entrance towards the back where the toboggan run headed downhill.

Sarah didn't even look for a helmet. She raced up to a toboggan, freed it from the snowbank, and signalled Travis to jump on behind her.

"*Nish!*" she shouted. "*Hurry!*"

Groaning and grumbling, a puffing Nish piled on behind Travis.

"*What're we doing?*" Travis yelled as the toboggan began slipping downhill and gathering speed.

Sarah shouted something back, but Travis only caught pieces of it:

"*. . . car . . . hill . . . cut them off!*"

18

THERE WAS NO POINT IN ASKING SARAH TO SAY it again. The wind blocked out everything but the hiss and scrape of the toboggan as it gained momentum under the weight of the three teammates.

They flew down the toboggan run, and then, with a sudden twist of her weight and a loud scream from Nish, Sarah forced them off the track and onto the fresh snow of the hill, heading straight down.

Travis could feel his heart pounding and knew that Nish was still screaming helplessly. He prayed Sarah knew what she was doing. Everything around them was a blur. They had no helmets. And they were hurtling straight towards the back road that wound its way to the highway and then to the interstate.

There were few cars on the twisting road, but Travis was still terrified. They could hit a car, a truck, a light standard. They could flip going over the bank and be left sprawling on the tarmac while cars and trucks skidded into them.

"*WE'RE GONNA DIE!!!!!!!*" Nish howled into Travis's ear. "*WE'RE ALL GONNA DIE!*"

Travis tried to shake off Nish's wailing. He looked up the road where it snaked down from Main Street and saw what Sarah was planning. The big black car, with dents along one side, was slipping and sliding down the hill, barely under the driver's control as he fought through the still-unploughed snow and slush from last night's fall.

Sarah's timing was almost perfect, and with a couple of twists of her body to take the toboggan on a slightly longer route, she quickly had toboggan and car lined up to meet just where the road dipped down and headed for the larger highway out of town.

"JUMP!!!" Sarah yelled back. "*JUMP!!!!!*"

Sarah and Travis left the toboggan at exactly the same time, Sarah spilling off to the right, Travis to the left.

The last sound Travis heard was Nish's scream as he sailed towards the road, holding on for dear life.

"*AAAAAIIIIEEEEEEEEEEEEEEEEEE!!!!!!!!!*"

"*NISH!*" Sarah screamed after him.

"*NISH!*" Travis shouted into the wind. "*Jump, you fool. JUMP!*"

But Nish held on.

He held on, screaming, as the toboggan dipped sharply, gathering speed, then swept up the embankment by the road, a perfect Olympic ski jump for the toboggan to launch from.

"*AAAAAIIIIEEEEEEEEEEEEEEEEE!!!!!!!!!*"

Sprawling in the snow, neither Travis nor Sarah could see a thing. Nish had simply vanished from sight.

And then came the sound Travis dreaded.

CRAAAAAAASHHHHHHHHHHHH!

19

"N–*I*–S–II–*I*–K–A–W–A."

Nish was beet red, his face glistening under the camera lights that bore down on him inside the mayor's office at City Hall. The mayor of Park City was standing beside him with his arm around the big Owls defenceman.

"That's *Nishikawa* – with two 'I's."

The mayor had just spoken to the assembled media – CNN carrying the press conference live – and had given full credit to the work of a peewee hockey team from Canada called the Screech Owls.

The Owls, the mayor had said, had figured out, and the police had confirmed, that Brody Prince had never been removed from Park City at all and was being kept virtually beneath the hotel in which his family had anxiously awaited word from his captors. The limousine and the helicopter had been diversions that might have succeeded had the Owls not found the secret hideaway.

The Owls also got the credit for linking the murder of Ebenezer Durk to the kidnappings. A forensic scientist working on a hunch had found traces of what appeared to be rainwater around Ebenezer's heart, but an analysis of the water indicated it had fallen as snow in the mountains, not as precipitation near the Great Salt Lake. The latest theory was that Ebenezer Durk had been stabbed to death with an icicle.

"*Latest* theory?" Sam whispered to Sarah and Travis, standing next to her at the City Hall gathering. "We were telling them that days ago."

But what really galled the three Owls standing there, watching the cameras move in as Nish spelled out his name, was that Nish had happily accepted almost all the credit for the daring capture of the kidnappers. It was Nish, seemingly all on his own, who had risked his life on a daring ride to send the toboggan flying into the black car, causing it to slide off the road in the deep snow. Highway patrol had immediately moved in to check on the accident, only to discover that this was much more than a mere fender-bender.

Nish, fortunately, had leapt free of the flying toboggan just before impact.

"*Leapt* free, my eye," said Sarah. "He *fell off*."

But no matter. Nish was the man of the hour, and the journalists were gobbling up this remarkable story of the heroic little Canadian who had saved the American superstar's child.

The Prince family had already posed for photographs with the hero, Nish with one arm around supermodel Isabella Val d'Or and the other around Troy Prince, the eccentric entertainer. All three were wearing sunglasses – *indoors*!

Travis noticed that when Troy Prince shook hands with Nish, the mega-rich superstar was wearing a see-through surgical glove. If Nish noticed, he never let on. He bathed in the publicity, letting the compliments wash over him like a warm and welcome shower. As far as Nish was concerned, he *was* the hero. The one who led them to safety after the gunfire in the tunnel, the one who directed the flying toboggan into the side of the fleeing car.

He even claimed, at one point, that the whole idea for the toboggan run came to him from Ebenezer Durk's account of delivering his daddy's moonshine in his little red wagon for the price of a chocolate bar.

Travis wondered if by now Nish would even remember the way it really happened.

He shook his head and chuckled quietly to himself. After this, Travis and Sarah would be lucky if Nish even remembered their names.

20

NOT ONLY WAS BRODY PRINCE OKAY – *HE WAS going to play!*

The kidnappers had treated him well. After they had learned the secrets of the tunnel from Ebenezer Durk, and then killed the old tourist guide to get him out of the way, they had quickly built a remarkably comfortable "cell" at the high end of the tunnel in which to keep their captive until the ransom was paid.

The plan had been bold. They had taken the youngster barely a mile, while police believed Brody had been spirited out of the state by helicopter. They had used Nevada telephones and addresses while making contact with the Prince family even though the heart of the kidnapping operation remained right in Park City.

The ten-million-dollar ransom was on the verge of being paid. The money had been assembled and a drop-off arranged – in far-away Reno – and had the Owls not stumbled upon the secret hideaway, the kidnapping would have been a total success. Brody Prince would have been found wandering the back streets of Park City the next morning, with the kidnappers long gone and the ransom money safely in the hands of their accomplices in Nevada.

Instead they were now behind bars. Three of the family's trusted bodyguards were included in the roundup and three others who were linked to organized-crime syndicates operating out of Las Vegas and Reno.

Brody Prince had been reunited with his grateful parents, checked over by doctors, interviewed by the police, and was now declared fit and ready to resume play.

There was, however, only one game left to play. The Hollywood Stars, playing without Brody, had gone on to tight wins over both the Vancouver Mountain and the Long Island Selects. There were only two teams with perfect records in the tournament, and organizers announced that these two teams would now meet for the gold medal.

It was to be played in the famous E Center, where Team Canada defeated Team U.S.A. for both the men's and women's gold medals in the 2002 Salt Lake City Winter Games.

And those two teams would be the Hollywood Stars, led by Brody Prince, and the Screech Owls of Tamarack, led by a big beefy-faced kid who kept saying "that's with two 'I's'" every time anyone spoke to him.

21

"HE'S DONE IT."

Fahd was beside himself.

"He's done *what*?" Travis asked as they filed out of the E Center following their only practice before the gold-medal game.

"He's buried something at centre ice, that's what."

"What do you mean, buried something at centre ice?" Sam demanded as she leaned across the aisle of the bus and into their conversation.

"Just what I said," Fahd answered. "Nish went and talked to the Zamboni driver, and now he's got something buried at centre ice for luck."

"What?" Sarah called over. "A loonie?"

"I don't think so," said Fahd.

"His boxer shorts?" Sam giggled.

"He won't say," said Fahd. "He just says he's done it and the gold medal is now a lock."

The four turned and looked to the back of the bus, where Nish sat beaming, his eyes closed as if in a trance, his smile almost wider than his big round face.

Sarah rolled her eyes and went back to her book.

There was only one evening left for Nish to complete the suspended Gross-Out Olympics.

He had raced through the remaining events – Sam losing the Alphabet Burp to a Coke-guzzling member of the Selects, Jesse coming third in the Chubby Bunny marshmallow chew, Liz volunteering for the Cricket Spit when no one else would, but losing, and Dmitri, as he'd predicted, running away with the Frozen T-Shirt event – and now the scores were being calculated by Data and Fahd to determine the medal awards.

Nish conferred with his scorekeepers before heading to the podium, a look of sheer delight on his face. As he reached for the microphone, Travis was convinced he saw the flash of a surgical glove beneath Nish's sleeve before the cocky emcee switched hands and turned on the mike.

"*Lay-deeees 'n' gennnullmen,*" he announced in his ridiculous Elvis impersonation. "Thank you . . . thank you very much. But we appear to have a tie for the gold medal."

The room went silent, as no one was sure what that meant.

"The Screech Owls and Panthers have exactly the same total points – and so we will move now to the special tiebreaker."

"What could be more gross than what we've already done?" Sam shouted, giggling.

Nish seemed enormously pleased at this question. He switched hands again, and this time Travis saw that he was indeed wearing a rubber surgical glove on one hand! Just like Troy Prince, his new idol.

Travis winced. If too much time in the spotlight had driven the likes of Elvis Presley and Michael Jackson and Troy Prince a little strange, what would Nish be like after a few more press interviews?

Nish turned to face the far side of the room. "Would you bring in the tiebreaker now, Fahd."

The doors to the ballroom opened, and Fahd, wearing a surgical mask, walked in carrying something on his back.

Not Fahd, too! Travis thought. *What was next? Sam acting like Isabella Val d'Or?*

"What is it?" Jeremy Billings of the Panthers asked.

"I have no idea," said Travis.

Fahd moved to the centre of the room and dropped what he was carrying onto the floor.

"It's a hockey bag!" one of the Stars shouted, obviously disappointed.

Nish cleared his throat into the mike. "Not

just any hockey equipment bag," he corrected. "*My* hockey bag."

"Open it and we're all dead!" moaned Sam.

"Jeremy Billings of the Panthers and Travis Lindsay of the Screech Owls, will you step forward, please?" Nish announced.

Jeremy looked at Travis. Both shrugged and stepped forward.

"You are each the captain of your team in the Gross-Out Olympics, so you two will decide the gold medal."

"What do we have to do?" giggled Jeremy.

Nish held up Mr. Dillinger's old pocket watch. "The competitor who can stick his head in the ol' Nishikawa hockey bag longest will win the gold medal!"

Nish stood back, grinning triumphantly, his red face like a beacon.

Jeremy was first to think of it, and straight away he said the two sweetest words Travis could have imagined.

"I concede."

22

"GIVE IT YOUR BEST," MUCK SAID.

That's it. Nothing else. He said this much and walked out of the room, then quickly came back in and looked around as if he'd forgotten something.

He said nothing. He simply let his eyes settle on Nish as he folded his arms and stared hard.

Nish broke into a full blush. "I know, I know, I know," he mumbled. "There's no 'I' in 'team'…"

"*BUT THERE'S TWO 'I'S IN 'NISHI-KAWA'!*" the entire team yelled out as one.

Nish only blushed deeper.

Travis pulled on his sweater, kissing the "C" as it passed. He had already hit the crossbar in the warm-up.

He knew he was in for a good one.

The E Center was packed. The people of Salt Lake City and Park City had come out by the thousands to see the finale of the tournament, though it was undeniable that they had come less for the hockey than for a glimpse of the kid-napped boy, the eccentric superstar father, and the gorgeous supermodel mother.

No matter, thought Travis, as he stood on his wing waiting for the puck to drop: the place was packed and this was going to be a game to remember.

Sarah looked up into the dreamy green eyes of Brody Prince, who winked. It was now Sarah's turn to blush. She looked down quickly and hammered her stick on the ice to hurry up the faceoff.

The puck dropped.

Brody Prince used Sarah's own special trick of plucking the puck out of mid-air before it hit the ice, and he gained control as he stepped around her and came straight at Nish.

Nish had seen the play and was already back-pedalling hard. He cut for the centre of the ice just as Brody came over the blueline and then went down neatly to block the pass as Brody tried to flip the puck to a flying winger.

Nish took the pass in the crook of his arm and scrambled quickly to his feet, letting the puck drop as he rose.

Brody Prince dove, swinging his stick to clip the puck away, and the puck flew up and over Nish, into the shin pads of the rushing winger.

The winger came in hard on Jeremy's short side. Jeremy pressed tight to the post, playing the percentages, and the winger delicately pinged the puck in off the far post.

Hollywood Stars 1, Screech Owls 0.

Nish was beating up on himself on the bench. He was punching his mask again and again and again. No one said a thing. They had seen this before. He was taking full blame for something that wasn't his fault at all. He had made a wonderful defensive play, only to have Brody Prince make an even more spectacular play, and the Stars had scored on a lucky shot. Mr. Dillinger calmly wrapped a white towel over Nish's neck and patted his shoulders.

Muck put Nish right back out next shift. He knew, just as everyone on the bench knew.

Nish was here to play.

There would be no "I"s in "Nishikawa" for a while, not until Nish had atoned for his error.

The Stars were an unbelievable team. They had size and strength and skill, yet still they depended on the trap system and used dump-and-chase more than any team Travis had ever played.

It made them almost impossible to play against, and it was difficult to get any flow into the game. If Travis or Sarah tried to carry the puck up through the middle zone, the Stars would form a blockade, forcing them to pass or circle back. The tactic was taking away Dmitri's fast break.

The Stars would get the puck and fire it along

the boards, then race in, hoping to press Jeremy into coughing it up, or else hammer one of the Owls' defence against the boards and get it that way. If this failed, they immediately dropped back into their trap mode.

Travis was exhausted, yet it seemed he had done nothing. There was no room to skate. No room for plays.

Muck was disgusted, but never lost his patience. He kept shaking his head at what he saw, but he would not let the other team dictate the play.

"Stay with our game," Muck kept saying. "Puck control is what works for us. Puck control and speed. It will shift our way."

But the Stars were up 3–0 by the time the tide slowly began to turn.

Troy Prince and Isabella Val d'Or were already on their feet and doing a victory dance when the second period ended, the score 4–1 for the Stars. The Owls would have been shut out entirely had a point shot by Sam not bounced in off the skate of one of the Hollywood defenders.

The Owls had only twenty minutes to come back. Travis felt antsy. Sarah was shifting fast from one skate to the other as they waited for the fresh flood. Muck, however, was perfectly calm.

"It's happening," he told them. "You might not see it yet, but they're tiring, and our skating is going to come through for us. Just you wait."

Muck was right.

The third period began differently, with the Stars relying on hooking and interference to slow down the Owls and the referee unwilling to let things go.

The Owls got a power play, and Sarah used her high flip pass to send Dmitri in on a clean break-away. Travis didn't even have to watch. Forehand fake, backhand high over the glove, the water bottle spinning off as Dmitri turned, his hands raised to signal the goal.

Travis then scored with the teams at even strength when Sarah split the defence and got in for a shot, the goaltender making a great sprawling save but the rebound perfect for Travis to chip home as he came in behind Sarah.

Hollywood Stars 4, Screech Owls 3.

The Owls were beginning to realize only a handful of the Stars – led by Brody Prince – could skate with them. Once Sarah and Dmitri turned it up a notch, and once good skaters like Travis and Nish and Sam and Jesse and Liz began using their speed and puck movement to keep the Stars back on their heels a bit, the game began shifting perceptibly to the Owls' advantage.

But dealing with Brody Prince was a different story. Travis found, in a race for the puck, that Brody could match him stride for stride. Brody was also much stronger, and if they reached the puck at the same time, chances were Brody would come up with it.

He was also fairly deft at puck-handling. Once – seemingly defying his coach's orders – he carried the puck the length of the ice, and had Nish not gone down spinning and knocked him off his skates, he might have been in alone on Jeremy with only a minute left in the game.

The crowd was calling for a penalty on Nish, but the referee refused to call one. Nish had been playing the puck, and the collision came after he had swept the puck away.

Troy Prince was on his feet in outrage. He threw off his headset and bounded down from the area in the stands his bodyguards – *new* body-guards, Travis noticed – had staked out. He began pounding on the glass.

The coach of the Stars, seeming to take his cue from the team owner, began screaming at the official. He picked up a white towel and waved it in mock surrender. The two assistant coaches followed suit.

Brody Prince, on the other hand, picked himself up off the ice, turned, and gave Nish's big bottom a friendly swipe with his stick blade, a sign of recognition that Nish had made a great play.

But an even greater play was necessary.

The clock showed forty-four seconds to go in the gold–medal game, with the Hollywood Stars up by a goal.

The Owls had forty-four seconds to score – or else.

Nish gathered up his gloves and stick, brushed off some snow, and skated slowly to centre ice, where he paused and very gently tapped the ice with the blade of his stick.

Travis watched from the bench. Nish was hoping for good luck, counting on his lucky charm – whatever it was – to come through in the crunch.

Nish's collision gave Muck time to rest his top line and have them ready to take an extended shift. He dropped Andy back from his usual forward position, putting him on the point with Nish in order to use his big shot.

Sarah took the faceoff, with Dmitri and Travis ready to go on the wings.

This time Sarah beat Brody to the dropping puck, plucking it away and onto Dmitri's stick. Dmitri sent it back to Andy, who immediately played it behind the net to Nish.

They had the puck where they needed it: on Nish's stick, with the rush about to begin. Nish stickhandled out slowly, weighing his options, watching for a breaking player.

Travis decided to gamble. He cut fast across

the centre red line, hammering his stick for a pass, and Nish hit him perfectly as Travis moved across centre, his checker moving with him.

Travis dropped the puck, leaving it for Dmitri, coming up fast, and Dmitri did the same for Sarah.

Sarah came in alone, one defender back. She faked the shot, the defence crouched to block it, and like a magician she slipped the puck between the defender's skates and out the other side.

Sarah flew in alone, deking with a shoulder and then rounding the goaltender to flick the puck over the outstretched glove and high into the netting.

The Owls bench exploded, players flying over the boards. Muck stared up at the scoreboard as if daring the numbers to change. He seemed to have expected nothing less than this goal. No cheering, no fist-pumping. Just the usual Muck.

The team pounded Sarah, and the referee had to threaten the Owls with a delay-of-game penalty to get them to return to the bench for the remaining twelve seconds of play.

Soon the twelve seconds were gone. The horn blew and the referee signalled sudden-death overtime.

Next goal would win the gold medal.

23

"THIS TIME."

Travis heard Nish speak but wasn't sure he understood him.

"You know what I mean," Nish said, then looped away from Travis's position on the wing. He skated over centre ice, right between Brody Prince and Sarah Cuthbertson, who were lining up for the faceoff, and as he went by he took off one glove, leaned over, and quickly touched the centre-ice dot.

"What was *that* all about?" Brody asked.

Sarah smiled. "Nothing – he's just an eccentric nut."

"He's a heck of a player," Brody said, bowing down to ready himself. "And so are you."

Sarah was speechless. She crouched down, dropping one hand low on her stick and reversing it to help her sweep the puck back if she could.

The ice had been cleaned again, a fresh sheet on which to write the final chapter of the Peewee Olympics. Sarah was glad it wasn't a mirror – she already knew how red-faced she must be.

The referee made sure Nish was back in position, looked towards both goaltenders to check that they were ready, and then dropped the puck.

Neither side won the draw cleanly. Sarah dropped a shoulder into Brody, and Travis jumped in to sweep the puck back to Nish. Nish dumped it up the boards, playing cautiously. The Stars dumped it back, and immediately fell into their trap positions without even trying to forecheck.

"We could play like this for a year and never score," said Muck, when Travis's line went off and Andy's came on. "I'd rather lose playing hockey than win playing tennis."

Travis thought he understood. Muck hated the style of play the Stars were using, and he'd rather go down playing the game he loved than succeed playing a game he loathed.

That was fine with Travis and Sarah and Dmitri – they didn't know any game but one that celebrated speed and puck control and smart plays.

The Stars' coach was double- and triple-shifting Brody Prince, hoping the elegant centre could find a way to score, but the result was an exhausted player who could barely drag himself up off the ice after he went down again hard.

When Brody smashed into the back boards, the groan Travis heard came not from the player but from the Owl sitting right next to him: Sarah.

Brody was nothing if not courageous. He fought as hard as he could and twice came close to scoring, one backhander clipping off the outside of the post when Jeremy misjudged his blocker.

"I don't want to win by a shootout, either," Muck said, barely loud enough for Sarah and Travis to hear. He was sending them a message.

Next shift, Sarah picked up a loose puck and circled behind her own net, looking for Nish. Nish, however, was just coming on to replace Fahd, and was in no position to take a pass, so Sarah decided to carry it herself.

She swung nicely around her first check and then came hard against Brody Prince, who tried to take her out with a shoulder, only to have Sarah duck under and away.

She was heading into the Stars' end, with Travis dropping back and Dmitri breaking. They knew to spread out. They knew to come in on a triangle rather than three across.

Sarah circled back, letting Dmitri head behind the net and watching Travis glide across into the slot, waiting for the pass.

"*With you!*" a voice shouted from behind Travis.

It was Nish. He must have cut across ice to the far side – way out of position – going deep along the side of the Stars' end, between Travis and the boards.

Travis knew that if he blew his chance and the Stars were able to cause a turnover, the Owls were in trouble. Nish couldn't have been more out of position if he'd been sitting in the stands.

Sarah's pass to Travis came quickly, sliding perfectly across, just out of reach of the last defender.

Travis raised his stick to one-time the shot.

The Hollywood goalie went down, anticipating, blocking all the angles.

Travis swung, deliberately missing, and then let the puck continue between his legs.

He heard groans from the crowd.

Then he heard Nish's stick strike hard against the puck, followed by the ping of hard rubber on metal.

Followed by the biggest cheer of his life.

Nish had scored on the Lemieux-Kariya play! It had worked!

Owls 6, Stars 5.

Gold medal to the Screech Owls of Tamarack.

24

TRAVIS HAD TEARS IN HIS EYES.

He was wearing a gold medal around his neck. He was captain of the winning team and his flag was being raised to the ceiling of the E Center while "O Canada" played over the sound system – just as it had for Team Canada in 2002 in this very same hockey rink.

The crowd had gone wild over Nish's goal. The media – many of them still lingering to cover the Prince family's reunion – had poured onto the ice and soon circled Nish and Brody, who had been named co-winners of the MVP award for the tournament.

The Owls had cheered as loudly for Brody as the Stars had cheered for Nish.

How things can change, Travis thought to himself. The one player the Screech Owls had hated was now one they admired the most. Sarah and Sam even had their pictures taken with him, and then the Hollywood captain skated over to Travis to ask if the two captains could have their pictures taken together.

Travis was delighted. But he was also puzzled.

There was still one unanswered mystery. And no one had made an effort to solve it.

What had Nish buried at centre ice?

The Canadian team did one victory lap of the E Center to a standing ovation by the crowd, and then, as they were gathering up their gloves, Travis found himself standing next to his old friend.

"You didn't dig it up!" Travis had to shout over the din.

"Dig what up?"

"The loonie – or whatever you buried at centre ice!"

"There was nothing to dig up," Nish answered.

"Fahd said you put something there."

"I did, but there's nothing to dig up."

Travis stood on his skates, blinking. "I don't understand," he said.

"I put *ice* at centre ice," Nish said, his big face reddening. "I melted down an icicle from the stables and I sprinkled it there for Ebenezer."

Nish shrugged and abruptly turned away, unable to say anything more.

And for the second time that wonderful night, Travis had tears in his eyes.

THE END

THE NEXT BOOK IN THE SCREECH OWLS SERIES

Attack on the Tower of London

The Screech Owls have won a contest that takes them to London, England, for a once-in-a-lifetime chance to play in-line hockey at historic Wembley Stadium. They leave the morning after Hallowe'en and arrive in time to celebrate Guy Fawkes Day in Britain.

But between trips to Madame Tussaud's famous Chamber of Horrors and the notorious Tower of London, the Owls become entangled in a plot so dangerous and frightening it makes Hallowe'en seem like a tea party.

Attack on the Tower of London *will be published by McClelland & Stewart in the spring of 2004*

THE SCREECH OWLS SERIES